Bardsy

2023 FALL ANTHOLOGY

FIRST CHAPTERS

Bardsy

Bardsy Press is an imprint of Bardsy, Inc.

23371 Mulholland Drive, Suite #446, Woodland Hills, CA 91364

info@bardsy.com

Published in the United States by Bardsy Press

Each author in this anthology is the sole copyright owner of the Work, and retains all rights to the Work except for those expressly granted to Bardsy, Inc.

To the extent a separate copyright attaches to the Anthology as a collective work, Bardsy, Inc. is the copyright owner of any such copyright on the Anthology as a collective work.

No part of this "Collective Work, or individual authors' "Works" may be reproduced, distributed, or transmitted in any form or by any means, including photocopying, recording or other electronic or mechanical methods, without the prior written permission from the appropriate copyright holder, except in the case of brief quotations embodied in critical reviews and certain other noncommercial uses permitted by copyright law.

Bardsy Press is a division of Bardsy, Inc. Bardsy is a registered trademark of Bardsy, Inc.

Correspondence regarding the content of this book should be sent to Bardsy, Inc., Editorial Department, at the above address. Requests regarding individual Works will be passed on to the copyright holders by Bardsy, Inc.

Publishers: Celeste Davidson and Adam Simon
Executive Editor: Celeste Davidson
Managing Editor: Casey Peta
Senior Editor: Pamela Raleigh
Graphic Designer: Aaron Weiss

Printed in 2023

www.bardsy.com

ABOUT BARDSY

Bardsy's founders are writers and educators. A lifelong bibliophile, Celeste Davidson always dreamed of being a writer. When her daughters were little, she couldn't stand how insipid most children's books were, so she wrote her own. Her debut, *One Leaf Rides the Wind* (Viking), was a bestseller that has sold over ninety thousand copies to date. Her most recent work, *Who Was William Shakespeare?* (Grosset and Dunlap), has sold close to half a million copies worldwide. Celeste, who also possesses MAs in teaching and educational research, and is pursuing a PhD in educational technology, has now turned to empowering other writers.

Meanwhile, frustrated by the limitations of his professorial gig and academic research, Adam Simon's interest in building community through storytelling led him to join forces with Celeste. Adam broke out his virtual hammer and built the website as Celeste developed a comprehensive approach to successful writing.

Bardsy, their brainchild, is a writing platform committed to helping you write more, write better and achieve the success you deserve. It includes an easy-to-use personal accountability system, clearly-defined benchmarks for evaluation of your writing, and a wealth of courses and resources. Elite members benefit from facilitated writing groups, an author website and professional coaching. Everyone has access to anthology contests, the fruits of which are shared in volumes such as this.

Join us at Bardsy.com

FOREWORD

If you're like the folks at Bardsy, nothing beats cozying up with a great new book. The first chapter of a new book represents the start of a journey to a unique place and time, offers a glimpse of compelling characters and foreshadows the themes and conflicts to come. Importantly, all great books begin with great first chapters: chapters that serve as a vehicle for the story.

On the flip side, a bad first chapter means the train never leaves the station. As we tell the writers in our workshops, readers need to climb on board from the first sentence, the first paragraph and the first page. Regardless of genre, it is up to the writer to make this happen, selflessly.

The simple truth is this: for a reader to appreciate a book, they need to read it first. Every book competes with the day-to-day demands on its reader: a full schedule, a family, a long work day. The same goes for agents, editors and publishers who deal with overflowing slush piles, exacting marketing departments and corporate bottom lines.

As you read the selections we have chosen as the finalists and winner of our First Chapter Anthology Contest, you will see how a variety of intrepid storytellers have learned this lesson. Each will grab you, regardless of genre or style. We hope you enjoy your time with Bardsy's latest batch of winning writers, and will follow them from the pages of this anthology to the shelves of your favorite bookstore. Their journeys, as authors, have just begun.

—CELESTE, ADAM AND THE ENTIRE BARDSY TEAM

TABLE OF CONTENTS

6 **Amber Baughman**
(winner)
No Hiding Place

20 **Stephen Bridger**
Frag

42 **Amanda Thompson**
Strata

56 **Andrew Ellingson**
Of Oaths And Ashes

76 **Stacey Campbell**
New Madrid's Fault

92 **Chloe McBride**
Better Off Dead

110 **Kate Altman**
The Luck Of Saints

126 **Erin Brashford**
The Scorched Sky

144 **Matt Bartle**
Photofit

166 **L.A. Redding**
The Time Between Us

182 **Jocelyn Coleman**
The Talish Trilogy: Changes

210 **Jo Ann Joseph**
Off Track

222 **Paula Bryner**
The Privateer

NO HIDING PLACE

By Amber Baughman

Winner

It was just before dawn and Alexander Clayton was on his way to a murder. He'd seen it from his house, a crimson stain in the western sky. Bloody and bright enough to bring him out at five in the morning – not that he had been asleep – and into the cold, sea-scented mist. He huffed his way through Black Cove, battered combat boots thumping on cracked blacktop as the whisper of the sea grew louder. It was close enough to dawn for the seagulls to quarrel, but far enough away that most of the houses Alexander passed were dark and still.

Alexander was no stranger to these dead hours. He rarely slept and the work he'd managed to pull together since returning to town–skulking, spying, and trespassing, the police called it–was often done best at night. But they didn't see what he did. The pain that

No Hiding Place

flowed out of the houses, the shadowy figures that fed on it. Sometimes he got paid for seeking out the pain and trying to find some way to quiet it. He might not have a license but the Cove was too small to sustain any sort of 'real' private detective. But even when he wasn't getting paid, if the call was strong enough Alexander couldn't help but tramp through the crumbling streets like the needle on a compass tuned to tragedy instead of magnetic north.

The red glow faded as he hopped off the road, squirmed through the brush, and slid roughly down the embankment to the shell-strewn coastline. He was hasty, trying to pinpoint the source before the dying light of pain and violence faded. He fell and cursed as he caught himself on the sharp edges of dead shells. The light of false dawn didn't yet reach the beach, and the thin, frothy wave caps were more visible than the black water they crowned; wild squiggles of gray that hung, spectral, in the air before crashing back into the tide. The beach had the familiar tang of rotting seaweed and heavy fuel oil; as the breeze from the water slapped him in the face, Alexander picked up undertones of coppery blood and the stink of spilled bowels. He sniffed the air in an unconscious, canine gesture and continued.

An untidy sprawl of flesh, dumped carelessly at the border to sea and land, was the fucked-up pot of gold at the end of Alexander's rainbow. He stopped well short to draw on gloves. Even from a distance he could tell there was no life remaining there, save a solitary seagull who fled with a strip of something in its beak. Evidence, no doubt. The beacon was only an echo, an impression birthed in terror by a desperate mind. Now dead and mercifully beyond pain.

He pulled a handheld voice recorder from the deep pockets of his army surplus coat. Unlike his clothing, it was sleek, new, and well-cared-for. Alexander checked the time on his phone before he thumbed it on. It took two tries as his fingertips tingled in the predawn chill of the air. "Five forty-eight AM." His voice cracked, rusty from disuse. "Body found. Adult..." he could only see the back and legs from this angle, but the shadows suggested broad shoulders and powerful thighs, clad in tatters of heavy denim and plaid flannel. "Adult male. Approximate time of death," he calculated back from when the beacon had given its last burning pulse, "five-fifteen AM."

He'd been a half hour too late. He scanned the coastline, but it appeared deserted and undisturbed except by the corpse itself. The rocky shore didn't take footprints. He didn't feel any other human mind nearby and the only sound was the heartbeat of the ocean crashing into the shore. "Suspect has fled. Cause of death?"

Now, he had to move closer. Water rushed around his heavy combat boots, but his feet remained dry. He couldn't say the damn things were fashionable, but they did the job. The flashlight on the cell phone was weak, casting deep shadows and washing out the colors even as mottled skin and glistening viscera took on shape. "Massive physical trauma. Thighs, genitals, stomach, and chest have significant laceration. Ribs–"

Here, even Alexander had to stop and suck in a breath. Someone had opened the man like some macabre flower. His head tilted back, dark hair studded with seafoam, chest flayed and cracked, ribs making bloody petals in the air except where they dipped into the water and were being washed to a stark white. As if that had not been enough indignity, the cavity formed by this had been filled with fruits and vegetables. They were stuffed so vigorously into the organs that only about half had spilled into the tide. The others remained, bulging from red and gray flesh as if they'd grown there. Bloodied cucumbers stabbed into the dense, dark flesh of the man's liver; oranges nestled like strange eggs in the dip between the lobes of his lungs. An apple, fallen from the body cavity into the surf, washed gently against a rib with every wave, as if seeking a route back inside.

Alexander swallowed to clear the nausea from his throat. His voice remained steady. "Massive physical trauma delivered to the torso, perimortem mutilation with foreign objects. Extensive damage. Death would have been fast. Cavity objects suggest the body was not dumped from a boat." He scanned the sea, anyway, but found no sign of a nearby ship. "Preliminary evidence suggests assault and death took place where the body was found." He rattled off the location for the record. His eyes kept returning to the rib cage. He'd seen objectively worse crime scenes – although not many. But something about the mutilation bothered him. He wasn't sure what it was and wouldn't be able to pinpoint it without a closer examination in better lighting.

For now, he took several pictures using his phone's camera. Not just of the body, but the surrounding area. A great deal of blood, but no sign of tracks, tools, or a campfire. The latter disturbed him the most; this wasn't the sort of work you wanted to do in the dark. If you even could. The gaping ribs suggested a monstrous amount of force. Where was the equipment?

People liked to say murder was senseless, but Alexander had never believed that. There was passion behind the taking of lives. It made an imprint on the world. If you could read it.

No Hiding Place

Alexander uploaded the photos to his server before tucking everything away in a deep jacket pocket. He settled into a half-lotus on the rocky shore, a good distance from the body. His palm throbbed; he pushed the pain away. His pain wasn't important right now.

He reached towards the corpse with his mind. *Give me your pain. Your sadness. Tell me your story.*

Terror swept Alexander away. He was stretched flat on the shore with his eyes locked on the uncaring sky above. *Was I drugged?* A distant thought, his analytical mind trying to make sense of the emotional impressions that lingered. Every muscle was slack, even with his brain screaming with the urge to flee. He could hear the crunch of her feet on the shore. The scent of her perfume faded into salt and seaweed. Her voice rose and fell in a lovely croon to the backdrop of the waves:

"Time is now fleeting, the moments are passing,

Passing from you and from me."

Memory and emotion this close to death was the clearest it ever got for Alexander; it was one of the few times he could read something like words. He fell deeper into the dead man's heart. Why was she doing this to him? He only knew her a little. He couldn't deserve this. No one could deserve this. What did he do? He tried to force the question through his lips, but they refused to move. He couldn't even blink. Please, he begged the sky and whatever cold God might lie beyond, whatever I did, I'm sorry. Please save me. The only answer was the gentle touch of her hand on his leg. Then, agony.

The pain started somewhere deep inside, like nothing he'd felt before. It clawed its way through him, rippling his skin as something inside of him cracked. He stretched until he could stretch no more. Inevitably, he tore, still trying to scream, to move, to do anything that might hold his rupturing body together. Everything he was spilled out into the night. As the pain and the darkness took him, he heard her sweet voice continue:

"Shadows are gathering, deathbeds are coming,

Coming for you and for me."

When Alexander clawed his way free of the memory there was vomit down the front of his shirt and jacket, and sour chunks lingered on his tongue. He rolled over and spat. It didn't help with

No Hiding Place

the taste of bile and last night's pizza but at least it cleared his mouth. He clawed at his coat until his shaking fingers found the phone. He only had three contacts and chose the first.

Natalie's voice was tinged with end of shift exhaustion. "Black Cove Police Department. How can I help you?"

"It's Alexander Clayton." Before she could hang up on him, he added, "I'm reporting a murder."

Two hours later, Alexander slumped in an interrogation room chair, eyes half-closed, trembling for all his attempts to soothe himself. The room was oppressive on multiple levels. It smelled like stale sweat and was soaked in fear and anger from previous interrogations. The emotional residue was impossible to escape, like he was soaking in lye. He tried to ignore it. A job made harder by the new, fresh waves of burnt umber contempt coming off the detective across the table. Anton Czerny was thirty-seven years old, with the build of a former football player who thought he could preempt the spare tires of oncoming middle age with enough stomach crunches. His dirty blond hair was starting to thin and when they had both attended the same high school, Anton had been popular in all the ways Alexander had not.

He watched Alexander with a familiar mix of pity and irritation. "Bullshit." His tone was weary. This was not the first time they'd gone over Alexander's story.

Alexander shrugged. "I don't sleep well. I walk sometimes. I found the body." *Like I said before, you complete asshole.* He pressed his lips together before it slipped out. His fingers tapped with an increasing urgency on the tabletop.

Anton didn't seem to notice–or maybe just didn't care. "Just stumbled across a corpse at five in the morning. By accident."

Another man, in other circumstances, might have responded that no one goes looking for corpses on purpose, but Anton had known Alexander for thirty years. Alexander didn't bother to pretend he wouldn't.

Instead, he opted for a certain degree of honesty. "It was a woman who killed him. I don't know who."

"Really? You saw her?"

"No."

No Hiding Place

Anton sneered. "Then how do you know it was a woman, Alex?"

"*Alexander.* I heard her voice."

The detective's gaze fell to Alexander's stained t-shirt and his lips curled with disgust. "You heard a woman. When?" Alexander didn't respond immediately. Anton answered his own question. "During a fit. Jesus, Alex. Your hallucinations are not fucking evidence. There's no way a woman held down a big, strapping man like that and tore him open. But you know who could have? Who has a history of violence? Of instability?" He leaned forward. "You're looking pretty good for it, Alex."

"*Alexander.* And no, I'm not." It was a growl. He hadn't meant it to be a growl. The room's anger, Anton's disgust, Alexander's own resentment and fear–they churned in his gut and expanded as if they might tear him open just as the man on the beach had been torn open. His fingers curled into fists, the fingernails biting into his palm as if the pain could help him hold on long enough to survive this interview. At Anton's snort, he continued as calmly as he could manage, "Look at my clothes. No blood. I didn't even touch the body. I preserved the scene. For you."

"Mmmhmm." *Pull the other one,* said Anton's derisive noise.

"You know I didn't kill him."

"Do I?" The detective's eyes narrowed. "Maybe I do, maybe I don't. But maybe I'd also prefer to have you cooling your heels in a holding cell while we make very damn sure you didn't kill him, and are, in happy coincidence, not running around like the lunatic you are and fucking with our investigation."

No. Holding cells seethed with nightmarish emotions. Alexander had seen enough of that. Felt enough of it for a lifetime. He didn't deserve this. He had been trying to help. "Anton, don't." His voice was strangled, more pleading than he wanted.

The detective stood. "You know the drill, *Alex*. Plan to be our guest for forty-eight glorious hours where we know where you are and that you're not getting into trouble." He made his way to the door, hesitating with his hand on the knob. "I'll call your father, let him know."

Pleasure. Anton's sympathy, such as it was, was only for Alexander's father–once upon a time, Anton had been a star halfback on the high school team, under the well-liked Coach Clayton. Alexander had not been on the team. For Alexander, Anton felt only contempt and a nasty pleasure at the distress the holding

No Hiding Place

cells caused. It sliced through the control Alexander had been trying so hard to maintain. Freed, the rage clawed its way to the surface. With a roar, Alexander lunged for Anton, teeth bared. The detective stumbled to one side, bellowing for backup as Alexander crashed into the door.

Anton retreated and Alexander pursued with handcuffed fists outstretched. Behind them, the door crashed open as two uniforms burst through. One slipped an arm around Alexander's neck and yanked him backwards, off-balance. The other reached for his sidearm. "Stop," snapped Anton. "It's just fucking Clayton."

He stepped forward to stare Alexander in the eyes. "You better hope I find a better suspect soon, Alex. I am tired of your bullshit. This town would be better off without you." Unable to breath, Alexander could only growl and jerk in the restraining grip, lost in anger and shame. Anton made a sound of disgust. "Throw him in the cell," Anton snarled.

They dragged Alexander out and no matter how he tried to explain, the words strangled in his throat as they turned to growls and animal noises of rage. Heads in the bullpen came up, saw Alexander, turned away. The whispers followed him to the cold, pain-soaked cells.

Bardsy 2023 Fall Anthology — First Chapters

"Crazy Clayton, again. Why don't they put him away?"

"You think he did it?"

"Who cares? It'd get him out of our hair."

Amber holds a Ph.D. in Counselor Education and currently works in the nonprofit research and evaluation field. She lives in the South, where she resides with family and the traditional writer's starting kit: far too many books and a cat.

No Hiding Place

FRAG

By Stephen Bridger

Njörn

Njörn should be master of all that he surveys, but instead he stands on the cliff-edge, broken by his sister's words: "You're a frag," she says. *A fragment of a human being.* He is left in no doubt as to the depths of her disappointment in him. This is the only thing which defines him in her eyes. She considers only those connected to be complete - linked by neural meshes to the wider world - *other people, other machines* - integrated in all things. For his older sister, Tove, this is the only way a Human should be.

And he isn't.

Frag

He stands, his body swaying, shivering, high above the sparkling waters of the lagoon below; the sky a pale pink which will darken to a more bruised lilac as the day progresses. He is the only one to come here since Tove left their island home for the Usk Academy a year ago. She was always going to fly away. *Always.*

It makes him angry she can only see him for what he isn't. And he hates that she's better than him.

At everything.

He takes one last deep breath and launches himself, arching his back, arms outstretched, legs together, fins pointed, diving in a perfect parabola, piercing the icy waters with barely a ripple. Long easy strokes propel him effortlessly into the labyrinth of gullies and caves; this is his second home. He is comfortable here, so focused on his hunt for the rivex, a shark-like creature, that he ignores the prickling sense of wrongness at the nape of his neck. Shoals of easganns and cuddies, tessellated orange and yellow fish which usually hug the eastern reef, dart in weird formations, startled and skittish; sand eddies swirl around him; eery high-pitched sounds register above the dull boom of more haunting resonances.

Flipping his fins, he torpedoes to the surface, unfurling the mask from his face. Smoke pours from the cliffs like treacle down the side of a tin; tendrils ooze over the lagoon towards him.

He catches a glint of flashing silver to the west, and when he turns, his heart lurches and pauses at the impossibility of the vision before him. He has seen them in the holos – the holographic movies. He would recognise them anywhere. *But they should not be here.*

He stares, disbelieving, as the silver fighter banks sharply, arrowing towards him. *A Cerulean jet!* Why would they attack? What possible reason could they have for being here, for hunting him down? He's a nothing. A nobody. *But their reputation…*every child on Praxos knows this – *ruthless killers, every one of them.* He fumbles for the connection of his mask, uncaring of the liquid trapped between mouth and filter, spluttering to inhale, desperate to submerge.

His only chance.

He plunges towards the wall of rocks, backing into the first cave he comes to, cloaking himself deep within its confines. The shimmering silhouette of the silver craft churns the waters above him. He struggles to breathe; his oximeter flashes its blood red warning. He only has three neurotoxic darts attached to his right

Frag

forearm: No match for a Cerulean or his jet. He's as good as defenceless.

Should he even try?

His parents are Keepers of the Gardens. They maintain the hydroponics, cultivate the algal vats, look after the simple mechanics of the orchard. They are not and have never been fighters. He cannot think of a single reason for this attack. Senseless and stupid. *Why* screams at him – *why, why, why*. And other *whys* come back at him. But he doesn't move; fear paralyses, overwhelms his growing, desperate need for oxygen, until he can hold on no longer, until he can't ignore his burning desperation. His vision dims, tunnels and darkens. *Now or never.* He shoots forwards, lunging into the water frothing around him, cresting the surface, gulping brine deep into aching lungs.

By luck, his timing's perfect. The jet ascends vertically. He watches it flash out of sight as it heads north across the island.

His island, his home.

The turbos have cleared the smoke in a circular ring, but with the jet's departure, the pseudopods of inky blackness slide back towards him.

He swims on the surface now. He should be relieved, but isn't. Now that he has time to think, he is overwhelmed by possibilities too awful to contemplate, and yet he can't stop himself. The dense smoke obscures the platform his father built into the tiny isthmus. His throat burns from the scorching bitterness of burnt plastics and partially combusted hydrocarbons.

He retracts his fins, then vaults the six steps to the platform, running to the shoot. The shoot flashes green. He leaps onto the pod, but the pod crawls.

Come on, come on.

Half the house collapsed, the space a mass of twisted metal and fallen masonry. He yells, but his screams echo back, unanswered. Clambering over debris, Njörn squeezes past a concrete buttress; the sight greeting him one of Armageddon - everything either on fire or smoking. Charred cereal, smouldering. Five of the six algal vats destroyed, the sixth oozes viridescent green through a jagged rent in its side.

He sprints the western trail to his mother's laboratory. She's linked

Frag

– she must have received sufficient warning. Must have escaped. Must have hidden. His eyes sting. Coughing and gagging, he strains to reach the last ridge. He imagines the geodesic domes, as if imagination alone can aid their power of preservation. But the evidence of streaming eyes confirms the domes have taken a direct hit. They lie shattered in a jumble of smoking wreckage stretching from the edge of the cliffs to the raging ocean below; whole panels smash against exposed rocks as if mere toys discarded by an angry child.

Njörn hunts through the wreckage. There's stuff here he hasn't seen before. *What is it doing?* They have no need for weapons, drones and cannisters with weird glyphs. This is a planet of peace. They've never been at war. But they're here, half buried in the mud, scattered amongst the foundations, and the cuttings and the plants of his mother's research. *What else have they been hiding?* But he suppresses the endless *whys* whirring inside him. His throat lumpen. He can't swallow. He grinds teeth together and presses on. He hunts for the only thing that matters. *Where are they? They must be here.*

It doesn't take long to find them: His mother's perfect face deformed and misshapen. His father's arms cradle her head. His left eye still open - Njörn's faint whisper of hope extinguished in a blink.

A shaft of metal pierces his father's belly. A trail of bent grass, and the crushed and broken stems of the lily-livered damsel flowers, tracks the path he has taken to drag them to this point.

His father sits with his back to the cliffside, his mother to his left. From a distance, it looks natural; as if they have done this a thousand times before - relaxing after a hard day's work, gazing into the western skies, the endless Pelarian ocean before them.

They have always loved him.

This thought should comfort but doesn't.

He wonders whether Tove is right - that he is not really a proper Human after all; that his incompleteness shields him from feeling as he should.

He closes his father's staring eye and rests beside him, facing seaward, trying not to look at the intricate metalwork within his mother. He doesn't cry. His thoughts turn so slowly it takes an age to contemplate something he should have considered earlier – much earlier: *His sister Tove must know.* She will have been

Frag

notified of his mother's death before him.

They're linked. He isn't.

Now, he's alone.

She will never be.

It's enough to make him howl; a bellow of inchoate, animal rage which has been bubbling within him ever since she first called him *frag*. His scream is swallowed by the waves smashing against the rocky shore. But it's always been there, within him; its heat and throbbing pulse, held close to his heart, nurtured and tended - its flame burning, ready to flare at an instant's notice, always waiting for that perfect moment to confront her with the injustice of his past and her treatment of him.

* * *

Tove

Tove would never admit this to her brother – she would rarely admit this to herself – but as much as she loves flying, as much as she digs being a cadet, as much as she accepts integration as the only way to function as a proper Human, her life isn't perfect. And sometimes, just sometimes, she needs to escape, switch off and recharge.

"We all require a hard reset from time to time," the Maester told her. "That's why we have the Dream Spheres. To help us remember where we came from. Sometimes we need to reconnect with what makes us, us."

If the lagoon is Njörn's special place, then the Dream Sphere is Tove's. She descends the stone steps to the inner sanctum - even the architecture based on the old world, an underground temple of symmetry and order, hundreds of colonnades crisscross the mosaic floor, bracketed torches cast flickering shadows, the cloying sweetness of incense mingles with the harsher smell of burning paraffin. Within each cloister – the space bounded by a square of colonnades – rests a freestanding bateau-styled copper bathtub with a vapour cloud above a pool of viscous dark-blue swirling liquid. She avoids the cloisters shrouded in darkness – these are

Frag

occupied.

She doesn't know whether the Dream Spheres choose her, or she chooses the Dream Sphere; each is linked to a different reality, a different experience, but the prayer engraved on to the side of every copper bath the same. They have all been taught to recite this childish rhyme to trigger the programme.

I am born of earth, of flesh and bone.

I swim in seas; I climb in trees.

And even though I have left you far behind,

I will always be Humankind.

Tove disengages identity and location before she immerses herself in the synaptic pool: This is the only place where she can be anonymous. In part, this is the point of the thing – to leave yourself behind – to forsake who you are now for what you once were.

She switches off her comms - except the emergency channel - discards her green jumpsuit and levers herself into the dark blue gloop, luxuriating in the immediate hit of heat and sensory distraction as her neural link embraces the connections freeing herself from her own limitations. *If it feels real, it is.*

She floats through wispy clouds and pale, blue skies, gravitating to the largest conurbation on the Eastern seaboard of a nameless continent. Her hair is braided, her skin pampered, her muscles massaged. She watches people on packed sidewalks churn through the chaos of rush-hour. She could watch this forever, mesmerised by the craziness of so many crammed into such a small space, and yet this was once her world. It makes her proud; to see where she has come from and the achievements of her race. It is obvious they would never have made it to the stars without order and integration.

Why would anyone reject this?

She feels pity for her father. He had to be severed from connection because his brain reacted to the trace metals in his neural mesh. But her brother defies comprehension. He has always been odd, but after his failure, she sees him as a lesser thing. He brings shame upon *her* family; makes *her* the laughingstock of the Academy.

A part of her will always be known as the girl with a Frag for a brother. And for this, she will never forgive him.

Frag

Only flying saves her.

Tove's parents named her after one of the ancient Terran goddesses, but she is more a spirit of the skies. When she first sees the summer gliders swooping over the cliffs of her island home, using the thermals and the swirling westerlies, she yearns to join them. It's dangerous resisting forces conspiring to drag you to your death - accidents inevitable - but this never puts dissuades her. Father observes from one cliff edge or another - mother hides in her laboratory or sneaks glances from behind her fingers.

Njörn ignores her. He would rather look at his own belly than the wider world.

But flying for Tove is as much a part of her as her neural link or the scar on her cheek from her first crash – or her short, cropped hair bleached by the summer sun – or her eyes; one as grey as granite and as fiercely unyielding, the other a softer mix of hazy green and light blue.

Tove makes it to her favourite place; she stands on a floating gantry linking the sky-tower to its first space-hub. The views are glorious, but just as she's about to jump, a flash of red rips through her vision; her mouth flushes with bitter tartness, her skin prickles from the cooling liquid around her. Buzzing torments her ears. She can't ignore these warnings.

She opens her eyes to fierce, blinding lights. Droning, blaring alarms - inside and out. She yanks herself from the cradle, gel slopping to the floor, fragmenting into globules which scatter in all directions. Her head muzzy, glitching from the wrench of where she is to where she was meant to be. Jelly legs, floppy arms, vision adjusting to the harshness of the real world.

No drills today. She's checked. Her mind catching up, her link syncing to something impossible – they are under attack. Battle stations. All hands to deck.

Shizzle's f'ing kingdom, she's the last to be notified.

She senses panic in her fellow cadets - their disbelief and fear, as if she's there herself.

Where are you? Jax already in the hanger, climbing into his jet.

Running down the eastern corridor, past the refectory, her stomach churning, her mouth dry. She can't remember dressing, but her jumpsuit tightens around her. She will need every ounce of

Frag

compression to withstand the enormous forces required for an emergency launch.

Her jet readies for action, canopy opens, turbos charge, but almost the entirety of her focus is on the squadron of Ceruleans – six silver birds flying in close formation, the shimmering remnants of their portal of entry still visible, plunging from the black vacuum of nothingness through the outer ionosphere, huge contrails of flames flaring in their wakes.

Thirty-three seconds to intercept.

Thirty-two

Thirty-one

By her calculation, she's out of time.

She can't make it.

Where are you? Jax's harness pins him to his seat. The sharp click as his canopy snaps shut. The howl as his jet prepares to launch. He's third in line.

Late as usual! Even at this moment Remus enjoys a dig at her expense. His thoughts jag and zip from angles of attack to projections of engagement; formations, all strategic - no whys, just aerial computations.

They are so different, but at this moment she would trust him - with her life if necessary. He's first in line – she shudders from the smash of G's as he rockets through the hangar's blast doors, ascending in a lazy arc into the lilac sky, followed by Ruby, Jax, Simla, Acton, Petrov, Margo, Yarg and Farrand - their thoughts merge and link seamlessly. This is Nexus Cadet Force Three. Complete. Except for her.

She Lags behind - her link not quite cut but stretching to breaking point; strands of fleeting connections; glimpses from multiple perspectives, all sharing the same determination.

To not fail.

To do our duty.

Tove buckles herself in. She nods acknowledgement towards Ground Control and awaits the signal for clearance; her screen a distraction as she witnesses the action above as Cadet Forces One

Frag

and Two make contact – twenty jets against the enemy's six.

It'll be over before she's off the ground; over before her own Cadet Force intercepts. But in the dizzying chaos of three-dimensional conflict, the Ceruleans triumph in every engagement. She counts four Cadet jets downed in less than the second it takes for her to scream out of the hangar.

She hurtles skywards, pressed against the seat, throat pulled into her stomach, eyes squished into the back of her skull, pulling nine, ten, eleven G's, vision narrowing, greying; dull black and paler scintilla explode in front of her.

She has been trained for this – hundreds of hours of sims - assaults on physiology and endurance; her body beaten and moulded to cope with extremes of disorientation - physical and mental stress beyond compare.

But this is real. This was never meant to happen. They're nothing more than a token defence, the maximum cadet force permitted under the Treatise of Planetary Protection. It doesn't make sense. There's nothing here.

Nothing.

This is a training base for Shizzle's sake!

She blanks - the tiniest of moments – a fraction of a second. The physics of centrifugal force – if she turns too quickly, blood squeezes to her legs, to her arms, away from her brain - but her automated compression should prevent this. Has it failed?

Her dash flashes, but she doesn't need symbols to inform her that she's diving, not climbing - spiraling towards the Pelarian ocean. The jet juddering and screaming, buffeted by forces threatening to tear her apart.

Has she been hit?

Impossible to have been out for this long, and not be warned.

She grips the steering yoke and yanks, straining every ounce of strength. She has crashed before, but only in a glider. Nothing can survive a collision at these speeds.

But this isn't what terrifies her.

Apart from the Dream Sphere, she has always been linked to people and the wider world - nurtured, informed and reassured. Even

Frag

when she sleeps, others sleep with her, share her dreams like she shares theirs.

And now there's only static.

Has she been abandoned?

Dead already?

Where are Jax and Ruby, Margo and Remus? Dead too? When she reaches, they.... aren't there. But her link can't have failed. She can still connect to her jet – sense altitude, ground and air speeds. Her link is working.

She spins toward the dirty grey waters - screaming winds, and screeching alloys and composites. She doesn't want to die alone, but her head is rattling, emptied of everything but herself. She screams. She sees the white crests now, the steepling waves nothing more than smudges, fast approaching, closer and closer, until the nose lifts, and the judder eases as she regains control; her jet levelling within a hundred metres of the ocean's surface.

Dumbfounded.

For a moment she considers this might be a trick – that somehow she's still within the Sphere. It's the only thing which makes any sense to her now - a type of neural exercise – a test of her combat readiness. A trial of her fitness for duty. Is she ready?

She has never heard of a simulation like this before, but maybe that's the point - it has to be unexpected to work. There can be no way in the real that Ceruleans would attack, would they? This must be just another induced delusion.

Until it isn't.

It can't be.

Nothing on her dash - no proximity warnings, no enemies nearby - yet there's a flash of silver to her left – a single Cerulean swooping towards her – gliding over the ocean, so close she can almost touch it. And in the distance – it can't be – the western cliffs of her island home, the domes glinting in the sun. But she's at least 2000 clicks away. She can't be here.

No time to react.

Too late to do anything.

Frag

Struggling to process what she's seeing; the burning laser blinds her. Everything flashes white and the next, black – obsidian and absolute, accompanied by a whisper so faint that she doesn't know whether she imagines it or it has been within her all along - *Love you.*

Love you.

Her mother's voice echoes through her, seamlessly twisting into every cell, every dendrite, stealing into connections she can never forget even if she lives another thousand years or a hundred lifetimes.

Tove experiences her mother's death as if her own.

It takes her a moment to understand.

She isn't dead, but her mother is.

Oh…

No words. No thoughts.

Through misty eyes, the empty vault of the horizon fuses with the

Pelarian Ocean. There is nothing in between.

Nothing.

Oh...

Oh...

Oh...

Stephen Bridger is a retired medic with loads of academic publications of little interest. He's spent most of his life in the south of England, working in busy hospitals, trying to support a family. Any time left over, he used to run, swim and sleep. He's finally woken up and started to release what's left of his dormant creative spirit.

Frag

STRATA

By Amanda Thompson

Everything has changed, and Duncan Ilwes is alone.

He stands on the edge of a ravine, the trench is barren of life and deep enough that the rays of the falling sun give way to shadows at the bottom. It's still too bright to hide the one thing that he thinks would be better off hidden.

It is an ugly, mangled thing, this corpse, which was moments ago a living, breathing human being with dreams and fears and beliefs and–*oh god. Charlie's dead.*

The thought settles in his gut like rocks scratching against his insides. His hands are still tingling from the shove, and he clenches his fist to feel something different. His can still feel the texture of

Strata

his best friend's shirt bunched in his grasp before he had pushed all of his weight into the boy, sending him over the edge. The adrenaline had made him clumsy, and he is still trembling.

He tries not to remember the gasp of surprise, the way Charlie attempted to twist around to meet his gaze for one last time before he fell out of sight. He clearly fails.

Time moves forward again. Duncan scans the area, eyes frantic as they sweep the forestry around him for any signs of life beyond himself. He cannot find any, no matter how many times he checks. His body refuses him any feeling of relief.

He sits himself on the edge, tauntingly close to the scuff of dirt and clay that would tell the story of how Charlie had tried to stay upright in the struggle.

Wait, was there a struggle? Duncan actually isn't sure anymore.

His arms shake as they press further into the ground, trying to find purchase in anything that could be considered real. He can't see Charlie's body from this angle, especially when he looks straight ahead. It's a small comfort.

He knows he needs to see it at some point. He needs to get close to it, examine it, memorize the broken points of the boy's bones and the minutiae of his final expression. He needs it like a widower needs that one last look.

And so he listens to the bombardment of thoughts begging him to *just go check the body already*. He stands on legs made of dough, a newly forming one-hundred-and-forty-five pounds draped around his shoulders, and he thinks he feels the grip of bony fingers digging into his shoulders. He shivers in the hot, dry air.

Duncan takes the long way down the ravine, turning back and walking a good distance until he reaches a familiar set of makeshift steps, flat slabs of stones perfect for climbing. He descends slowly and mechanically in a waking sleep. He thinks of nothing, sees nothing, hears nothing. The only thing he can register now is his heart in his esophagus threatening to leap out and fall into a busted heap onto the steps. He almost wishes it would happen.

The closer to the bottom he gets, the more the sensation grows. His mouth waters as there is a faint smell, the process no doubt sped up by the summer heat. He wants to vomit, needs to get this awful

Strata

feeling out of his system. He can't face this reality if he feels like his body is about to implode on itself, but instead, his health persists out of spite. Physically, he is fine.

He no longer has the luxury to dwell on his own bodily sensations, however, finding himself standing before the body of what used to be his dearest friend. Duncan takes in the dark hair mottled with blood, a halo of red turning a tarred black as it pools around the head. One arm is curled under the torso while the other is splayed out, depicting a visceral break, the forearm almost completely detached from the rest. It only hangs by a small stretch of muscle.

Duncan crouches next to him–"*it,*" *not* "*him,*" he reminds himself–peering into the only accessible eye left intact with Charlie's skull, the other one hidden behind a stray web of curls and blood. It doesn't look lifeless like the books and noir films from his youth taught him. No, it looks like Charlie is staring straight back, reaching a depth Duncan could have never appreciated before this moment. He wonders what Charlie would say now if he could say anything. Duncan's own vocal cords tighten as he fights to breathe, and he doesn't recognize the stinging in his eyes before the tears have already blurred his vision.

It's not fair. The voice buzzing through his head sounds oddly like

Charlie. *It's not fair.*

He stays there until his tears dry and the sunlight falls enough to cast a shadow on the both of them. It wraps around Charlie like a blanket, Duncan thinks. Then he heads home.

※ ※ ※

Dinner is easy. He has at least that long before everything goes to hell. If someone discovers Charlie at the bottom of the ravine tonight, he likely has another hour or so before the authorities come busting down his door. He didn't think this far ahead, about the consequences, about what would happen to him afterward. It's not as though he woke up earlier this morning and thought, *I'm going to commit murder today!*

Duncan had seen something strange there for months now. There was a change in Charlie, beginning at some point that Duncan was never able to figure out. He had become terser, quicker, more solitary. Or at the very least, he had been pulling away from Duncan, and that stung. They had been brothers for over a decade, friends even longer, so one would think that their bond was stronger than this. Duncan had been feverish trying to win his friend back for weeks, but the harder he tried, the further Charlie pulled away. Charlie was becoming something foreign, something uncomfortable, and Duncan could tell their friendship was on its last legs.

It was in the little things, like excuses to miss meetups and the dwindling contact. Charlie rarely even spoke to Duncan these days, and it mystified him. The change couldn't have been as sudden as it seemed, but Duncan couldn't for the life of him pinpoint where it had all gone wrong. Duncan couldn't win. So he lashed out.

Now he's here, and Charlie is gone.

***

It's several hours later as he lies in bed, with no word of anything out of the ordinary, that the worry begins to get the best of him. Tired of phasing between awareness and mental static, he forces himself to focus on his surroundings, a technique taught to him years ago by his childhood therapist. He is in his bedroom, under the duvet, facing the ceiling, hands tucked behind his pillow. He rubs a finger along the fabric of the pillowcase, noting the friction of threads against the ridges of his fingertip. There's the faint smell of wet wood that has permeated the room for as long as he can remember. There are all things he can confirm. These are all things that feel normal.

His eyes adjust to the darkness, and he watches as shadows dance ominously around his room. They were frequent visitors of his. Before, these same shadows used to cast a certain twisted levity to his dreamless nights, or at the very least acted as neutral spectators watching over his subpar sleeping habits. Tonight, however, they are veiled by an aura of malice. It's a trick of the mind, he's sure, but that doesn't keep his heart from racing when the shadows grow closer only to draw away, pulsating to some sort of unfathomable rhythm.

He's half convinced that he's dreaming when the shadows collide and gather around his bed, only to dissipate seconds later and gather somewhere else. His body fluctuates between unbearable waves of hot and cold, and he fights with his covers every few minutes as he tries to force himself to settle down.

Duncan squeezes his eyes shut, helpless to the blues and purples that spread across the darkness, until finally, they turn into a hot white, and his eyes begin to ache. Reopening them, he stares into the void as his vision adjusts yet again, the colors depleting dot by dot, needle by needle, and then he's back to square one.

Strata

His mind would like to be cruel to him for what he's done. It shows him images of Charlie's face, plays clips of Charlie's fall like a sick movie. He sees Charlie's face, hears the sharp gasp of surprise, feels the weight of his friend disappear into nothingness. Duncan had wondered if there was a struggle before the fall; now, with all the clarity of someone looking back, he knows there was no fight at all.

Charlie had trusted him, and a lot of good that did him.

Duncan is hit by everything he refuses to acknowledge, and he is teleported to that rock formation once more. The heat of the afternoon sun radiates on the back of his neck, and his mind's eye paints the watercolor orange and yellow and pink that swirled in the sky as the sun crept lower. He can recall the sensation of his hand against cotton warmed by skin and cooled by sweat, and the amount of force he had to exert as he pushed, surprisingly small for such a drastic result. He can inhale the strong earthy smell of dirt and pine trees. He thinks of a moment he had in the aftermath, standing there, watching a couple of birds flying overhead, their vectors of flight intertwining as they twisted around each other and clashed before splitting away and coming back to do it all again. To be those birds, he had thought, flying and surviving, nothing more. It would be so much easier than whatever this awareness is, he thinks.

And it repeats. Over and over again, he replays the events in his head obsessively, and with every time, he notes more and more made-up details, no doubt his brain attempting to erroneously fill in whatever blanks it could. The overpowering smell of iron wafts to his nose, and his eyes snap open, no longer to complete darkness. When had he closed his eyes?

The light of morning is just beginning to filter through the window. The shadows are long gone. Did he fall asleep? Could that count as sleeping? He doesn't feel well-rested at all. Awake and undressed, he sits in bed with an unnamable dread forming in the pit of his stomach, rendering him immobile. He soon resigns himself back to the comfort of his sheets despite their being drenched in sweat. It's all he can do, to retreat, before the inevitable happens.

Except that nothing happens today either. There are no blaring sirens as he showers away the filth of yesterday, no cops kicking down the door as he fixes himself a bowl of cereal. The morning dips into the afternoon and lunch is being put away when he decides to take action.

He can't just sit still and go about his day as if nothing happened.

Instead, Duncan straps on his filthy hiking boots and fills a canister

Strata

of water. He sets out in the early afternoon, the sun's wrath beating onto his entire body as he treks, slowly, casually, toward the scene of the crime.

His boots grow heavier with each step, and it feels as though he is treading through a pool of molasses the closer he gets. What if the police were there this very moment? He would without a doubt look incredibly suspicious.

But he doesn't care. There is something nagging at him, tugging at the edges of his brain, yelling at him to *confirm, confirm, confirm!*

Duncan walks, and walks, and walks. He barely pays attention to where he's going at this point, meandering along the path he's been down so many times that he automatically registers the landmarks as he passes them. First there's the climbing wall, a large sheet of red rock and clay with sharp stones jutting out at sporadic intervals. He and Charlie had climbed that very rock numerous times, pretending they were adventurers running from some dangerous beast when they were younger.

Next comes the brief canopy of bent trees, their trunks leaning over the edge of cliff-faces above him. Duncan remembers the first time he had explored that forest. It had always been there, just a short way beyond his house, but he was always too scared to enter. It was vast, and the shape of the trees made him inexplicably uneasy. It was only when Charlie begged and yanked him by the arms that Duncan had hesitantly agreed. With Charlie, the trees weren't strange or creepy; they were interesting, mysterious. Soon they frequented that forest more often than they frequented the nature trail below. Duncan still didn't know what they were or why they became like that, but Charlie had apparently looked into it after the first visit. "These are trail trees," he had explained. "My dad says that the Native Americans made them that way so they wouldn't get lost."

"How did they get the trees like that?" Duncan had asked, becoming extremely invested in learning more about the trees. He recalls how Charlie's face had fallen into one of dull realization.

"Oh, I forgot to ask." It was funny then, a silly little memory, but Duncan can't help but feel sour about it. Everything regarding Charlie feels sour now.

Finally there are the infamous steps, the layers upon layers of stone that led to the top like a staircase. Duncan remembers the first time his mother had brought him here, enthusiastically showing him "nature's wonders" as though the steps had been formed naturally.

Strata

He hadn't known whether it was true back then, but seeing the sparkling gleam in her eyes and her wide toothy smile, he would believe anything she said. She only ever held that radiating joy when she was in nature. Back then, he could earnestly believe that this was where she belonged, that she was born from a spring in the middle of the woods or from the bark of a tree, like a fairy. Unfortunately, this was long ago, and she doesn't go outside much anymore. She still has a small inkling of that dazzle, especially when he tells her stories of places he's visited, but it's not the same.

Wait.

His heart plummets. He is at the steps. These are the ones, right? He examines them, and whirls around to behind him, rock and sand over the horizon. Nothing else. He should have passed the body by now.

Has he not been looking carefully enough? Certainly a body is too large to just gloss over. He starts walking back the way he came, more carefully combing the area for even the slightest spot of blood. He can't control his breathing. His chest feels so heavy it might actually burst this time.

He begins jogging, searching more frantically, until he's running, sprinting, breaths coming in small pants as his eyes dart to the spots where the body could have, should have been. He only slows to a trot when he sees his house in the distance, a clear sign that he's gone too far. He stops in his tracks and the world spins around him.

There is no body. Nothing is here but Duncan, the rocks, and the skies that watch him.

Amanda is a grant writer by trade but is currently branching out into writing fiction. As a horror enthusiast, she writes primarily in horror and magical realism.

OF OATHS AND ASHES

By Andrew Ellingson

"To become Blooded is the highest honor on the continent of Helosia. For an Oath of Blood is a solemn promise, an admission to service and an unbreakable resolve. But, above all, it is a declaration: death can wait."

-Yavin Cleareye, Necromancer of Adin,
Royal Blooded of Nimandia

Chapter 1—Parley

The legionnaires and outlaws staring each other down had been at war for so long, few of them bothered to ask why anymore, and even fewer managed to care.

After nearly a century of bloodshed, it was known that the legionnaires were the rightful predators, and the outlaws were the reluctant but deserving sacrifice, those still paying for the sins of men and women long since wiped from the world.

At the head of his legionnaires stood the captain who had led them into such a harsh part of the continent. He kept his hands at his side in the secluded cavern, observing his country's forever enemies.

The Banished. Outlaws. Wild killers. Descendants of traitors. They were those sentenced to wander the mountains and die in the process until the end of time. They prayed to everything, to anything, that their penance would one day be paid.

It would not. Not while he lived.

Banished people were dirty, largely uncivilized and in some pockets according to rumors, cannibalistic. A far cry from what their ancestors had been, to be sure. But they were hard as iron, and they survived against insurmountable odds. As such, they had the captain's respect, though it did nothing to dull his hatred.

A few moments later, the Banished parted for one of their own. The woman who stepped forward had dark, brown hair that had been tied off at the ends and hung down to her waist. It was freshly washed. Even in the dim light of the cavern that they had agreed to meet, he noticed the sharp eyes and high cheekbones. She could have been considered pretty by some, but the harsh mountain range she was forced to call home was etched into her very features, and it was not forgiving.

No, she was not pretty—she was the picture of cold determination and ferocity. Unyielding, as beautiful as cold stone and snow. She raised a brow at him, her eyes flashing. "And who, may I ask, is the man that ventures this far into my territory to treat with me?" she purred.

The captain nodded at the woman, surprised by her eloquence. "Dyko Reen of Messtos, my lady. Son of Jiyko Reen, Royal Blooded of Demach and His Majesty Yuzzaf Kamal."

Of Oaths And Ashes

There was a snickering from some of his soldiers at the proper introduction to one they considered worth less than dirt. Dyko snapped his head around, and their chuckles choked under the intensity of his stare. There was little time for that.

Dyko turned back to the woman. "If I may?" he asked, gesturing to a large rock that he fancied as his seat.

The Banished woman nodded, and her eyes lingered. Dyko made a note. She recognized his name. "If you must."

Dyko folded his thin arms over his chest as he sat, silently wondering if this was the woman who had decapitated three of his emissaries in the weeks prior to the meeting. It had taken quite a bit of persuasion to gain an audience with her, as it had been with the other villages he had already visited. The meetings were delicate; they had to be done with words, not weapons.

"And I may address you as..?" Dyko asked, removing a flask from his waist and taking a strong sip.

The woman snorted. "Does it matter?" she asked.

"It does to me."

"I disagree."

He frowned. "Pardon? I have dedicated my life to being respectful and courteous. It is how I was raised."

"Raised? I was under the impression a blood demon shit you out." She raised her arms wide, glaring at him. "Did your parents teach you how to pound nails into wood, too?"

"Yes. My father was raised to be a carpenter before his service began."

"In that case, your father must be very proud. A son grown in his very image."

Dyko tilted his skinny head, blinking dark eyes set under bushy eyebrows. Her references were clear. "You still have not given me your name," he said.

"You may call me Quentessa," she said without emotion.

Dyko smiled at the concession. She had to be in her forties or fifties, but anyone not familiar with how the Banished lived would have mistaken her for seventy. Wrinkles and scars were

Of Oaths And Ashes

easier to come by in the mountains that cut across the middle of the continent. So too was frostbite, mutilation and death. "Right then, Quentessa. I must say, you speak remarkably well for a Banished," Dyko said.

"Thank you. You are remarkably civil for a murderer."

"May I ask how you have become so fluent in the continental tongue?" he asked.

As far as he knew, the Banished spoke some semblance of the common language, broken and fragmented as it was. In pockets, they spoke their own language altogether. This woman, with her knowledge, was an anomaly.

She raised an eyebrow, pleased. "You may not."

Dyko frowned. "I hardly think—"

"But I suppose I shall tell you. I do not spend all my time in the mountains." She leaned back. "In fact, I have spent much time in your home of Messtos. And other places. In those travels, I have learned."

"I see." Dyko's king had long feared the Banished had quietly assimilated into their cities. They had made a point to find these outlaws, but it was a large continent. They couldn't catch them all. "And other cities?"

Quentessa smiled, but she did not answer.

Dyko shrugged. "Well, if you must infiltrate society, I prefer it to be all corners. Not just the ones I hold dear."

Quentessa snorted again. "Infiltrated. What a word that is. As if you and your kind are not those that drove us away."

He scratched the tattoos on his hands. The one on the top of his hand indicated his rank, and the ones on his fingers had been given as merits for his service. He had accomplished much to earn them, but this mission was to be the final piece. The final test. He yearned to give his Oath. "Yes, well, those are nightmares of the past." He opened his palms. "I offer dreams of the future."

Quentessa looked at his waist. She opened her hand and waved it forward.

Dyko unhooked his flask and tossed it to her. Quentessa

Of Oaths And Ashes

caught it and took a long swig, not even flinching at the strong spirits that left greater men and women teetering on their feet. She tossed it back. "Do begin, Dyko. My men are restless."

He folded one leg over the other. "I will be short. I am here on behalf of my king, the deserved King of Helosia. He seeks an alliance." He eyed her soldiers. "Your people know these mountains better than any other. That is an advantage. An advantage we would like access to."

Quentessa blinked. And then she blinked again, processing. She looked much like an owl in the shadows of the cave. "You understand we have heard this lie before, yes?" she snarled, unable to hide her disgust.

He put a finger up, leaning forward. "Perhaps before. But not now. The Tribunal Accords were long ago. The alliance between my country, Nimandia and Amala wanes. They are not our enemies. Yet. But my king is proactive, and he is humble enough to admit when he needs help."

Quentessa barked a laugh. "Yuzzaf Kamal? Humble?" She laughed again, and the entirety of the Banished host did too at her lead. "Please, Dyko, I did not know you were such a jester. What other skills do you possess?"

Dyko bristled under his skin at the insult to the king he loved. All his life, he had only meant to serve. His king. His country. His father. "Many. As does my king. And he will keep his word."

"The continent has never had one, single king." She waved a hand dismissively. "Your king is not fit to be the first. He is as much a tyrant as Lightblood and Illian. Three countries, three rulers"—she frowned—"all murderers."

"My king has a vision to see our continent united as one country under one flag instead of divided amongst several. Division creates unrest. Unrest is...impractical compared to order."

"I suppose that is one way to put it," Quentessa grumbled. She stared at him. "What are you offering us in return for this...help?"

"In exchange for discreet passage to establish a strategic advantage against our enemies, we offer you your land." He blinked. "And the impunity to wage war to take it as you see fit."

Quentessa's face twitched; she couldn't help it. To return to their homeland was the only thing the Banished *truly* wanted in the world. Well, that and the murderous rampage of revenge. "All of our land?" she asked.

He shrugged. "Some of it."

"Some of it is not enough."

"It is all I have to offer."

She sat in silence, pondering. Dyko didn't like being on the defensive, and for the lull in their conversation, he was at the mercy of her mind. Seconds moved by as he counted. Then a minute. Then another.

Quentessa clicked her tongue. "Well, Dyko, I have thoughts. The first: may I call you by your *true* name?" She narrowed her eyes and waved him away. "Forget my question, actually, I care not for your permission."

She jabbed a finger at him. "You, *Son of Splinter*, are a savage. I am surprised I took your audience, as I tend not to speak with savages. *Especially* one who nails my people to crosses by the hundreds with such merciless wrath that the wood splits and splinters." Her lips curled in a sneer. "Your father clearly taught you well."

She spat the alias at him like one would spit out spoiled fruit.

"Tell me," she continued, "was it some childhood trauma that propelled you to inflict such pain on other people as a way to feel powerful again?" She snarled as she mocked him. "Did some perverted adult in your life play with you in inappropriate ways? Oh, no, I know, you were rejected often by those you chose to pursue romantically—"

The entrance to the cavern suddenly exploded in a shower of powder and blood. Dyko was thrown from his seat. Limbs of his legionnaires stationed near the entrance were ripped clean off, slapping against the walls with wet *thumps*. Bodies were thrown off their feet with such force it was as if they were nothing more than dolls being tossed aside by a bored child.

And then came the killers.

Dyko groaned as he turned over, shaking his head. It was thumping something terrible at the base of his skull. He reached his hand up toward his neck and pulled it back, finding the dark blood on his fingers.

Of Oaths And Ashes

One of his men appeared over him, a face wild with fear. "Up, sir, get up!" He reached a hand down to Dyko. "We have to move—"

A bullet tore through the man's neck, silencing him. He hit the ground, his dead eyes coming to rest just a few inches from Dyko's face. He pushed the man away, snarling as he reached for his weapon. But, before he could, a heavy boot stomped down on his hand, shattering it.

Dyko hissed in pain, daring to look up only to be met by a massive fist that hit him square in the jaw. Dyko laid flat on his back, his head swimming, as the boot moved to his chest.

Dyko could do nothing but flail his arms out in surrender, closing his eyes as he listened to the slaughter. Demachians yelled for each other in desperation. The Banished hollered in their own language. Chaos infested his ears.

The heavy boot on his chest released, and Dyko opened his eyes as a massive body walked away. He could not move after it, though, as the tip of a sword appeared at his throat. He glared up at a hooded figure, feeling the blood in his mouth start to dribble out onto his chin.

Dyko dared to shift his eyes to where Quentessa had been sitting. She must have betrayed him. Given up her honor of parley. He should not have been surprised. She was Banished, after all.

But if he was to die by her hand, he wanted to watch her do it.

Instead of finding her smirking over him in victory, Dyko was surprised to see her in the same position he found himself in. Wounded.

Quentessa was in the corner, not far from her seat for their meeting, surrounded by at least a half dozen dead Banished who had clearly tried to protect her. Her right leg was mangled, and her left shoulder sagged from a wound. She was staring up at a body. A very large body.

Complete and utter fear infested her eyes as she spoke in a hushed tone.

And when the body turned, removing the hood over its head, Dyko felt his heart stop.

Oh, fuck.

The giant man approached, thick beard spotted with blood, looking around as Dyko heard the killers rummaging through the pockets of his dead legionnaires. Damn them. Damn them for that.

A man of pure mass and ruthless reputation came to a stop above him, and the soldier with the sword pulled back, sheathing the weapon. He walked away.

Dyko spit blood, staring up at the giant standing over him. "Nimandian," he growled, refusing to use the man's name, though he very well knew it. Everyone on the *continent* knew it. Nimandia, the northernmost triplet of Helosia's established countries, was filled with killers, and this was their talisman. Their Blood Commander. Dyko tried to cough away the pain in his chest. It was no use.

"Demachian," the giant sighed back. "You should not have come here."

"Someone had to."

"Incorrect." He looked around the cavern. "This is treason. You spit on the laws of the Tribunal."

Dyko chuckled. "That is a matter of opinion." He struggled to perch himself on his elbows, though one of his arms was screaming for relief. Broken, then. He breathed through it. "So, what now? You take me to the Lightblood for questioning? To the torture chambers that are so famous?" He tried to hide his fear in his words, though it was very much real. "Please, take me. My fate does not matter."

The giant man blinked. "Many say that." He licked his lips. "Many lie."

Dyko looked around at all the bodies. He could smell the stench of gunpowder and blood. He was used to it, but this time, it shook him more than he wanted to admit. Failure was a foul smell. "This meeting is one of many. You cannot stop it," he said, baring his teeth, attempting to take back some semblance of control. "The pieces are in place, and you are one man." He grinned. "If my king burns, so does your queen."

"I am aware," the Nimandian growled.

Dyko had been in rooms with this man before. He could hardly believe that his father had marched alongside such a monster all those years ago. Fought with him. Nearly died with him at Kalizan.

Of Oaths And Ashes

His sheer size had always fascinated Dyko, as had the tattoos that ran wild over his skull and neck.

But it was his eye made of iron that had made him so famous.

"Nimandian!" a desperate voice called out from their right. Dyko found Quentessa breathing heavily, her body still mangled and useless. "I have information!" Her eyes betrayed her for a moment, glancing off into the corner. "For a price, I will tell you."

The Nimandian slowly shifted his gaze, leveling one eye at his prey. The iron in the other socket was dark and cool, without an ounce of sympathy. "No, not you," he said.

A Nimandian legionnaire quickly pulled Quentessa's hair back and slit her throat without a word. He pushed her body to the ground to let her bleed out. The giant Nimandian commander flicked his head to the corner that Quentessa's eyes had dared to venture to. "Bring that one."

Dyko heard grunting and watched as Nimandian legionnaires pulled a body from the shadows. The body tried to struggle, but it was no use. Dyko noticed it was a boy that couldn't have been more than twenty, and his terrified eyes disappeared as the legionnaires tossed a hood over his head.

The Nimandian Blood Commander turned back. Dyko offered a grin. "Truthfully, I believe the warmth of a prison will be a welcome distraction after so many cold months—"

"Nor you."

A Nimandian legionnaire, his face blackened with soot and blood, stepped in front of Dyko and crouched down, close enough so Dyko could smell his rancid breath. The soldier turned his nose up. "You dishonor your ancestors," he snarled.

An honorable death would have been a decapitation. The blade slammed into his gut and with a gasp, Dyko felt it ripped violently sideways and then back out. He pitched onto his shoulder, his life leaking out of him, as the Nimandian legionnaire wiped the blood on Dyko's uniform before standing up and pacing away.

Dyko's vision began to blur. His strength fading, he watched the Nimandian Blood Commander look once more around the cavern. He cracked his neck. "Cut off the brands. Burn the bodies. No evidence," he growled and immediately turned on a heel. "We leave in five minutes."

Of Oaths And Ashes

"Where to, sir?" Dyko heard one of the legionnaires ask as he gasped his last breaths.

"Home. Our queen. War."

Born and raised in Minnesota (the North, mind you, not the Midwest), I'm not sure what to put here, honestly! I've been loving and writing stories since I was a kid, and even back then, when my writing wasn't any good, I just wanted to put all the worlds and adventures in my head to the page. My mother instilled in me a love for fantasy and fiction from a very early age, and it's the greatest gift she's ever given me.

When I'm not writing, you can find me on the golf course with my longtime friends or watching whatever Minnesota sports team is playing-- here's to hoping the Vikings, Wild, Twins or Gophers win a title sometime soon!

Of Oaths And Ashes

NEW MADRID'S FAULT

By Stacey Campbell

Biscuit, 1968

1

The familiar clanging of keys and the metallic scrape of bars sliding into their casings breaks my focus, causing me to place my freshly sharpened No. 2 pencil (that has not been used enough to even be slightly dulled yet) down onto the tiny oak desk where I sit and next to the freshly opened, thick-ruled, 100-sheet notebook into which I have barely managed to write my first, small paragraph. I look to the source of the sound and see Tellie and his new partner standing in the open door to my cell. A tiny, scared woman clutching bedding to her chest huddles between them.

New Madrid's Fault

Apparently, this is going to be my new cellmate.

Ah, shit.

I don't use a lot of swears, hardly even think them due to how I was raised, but this definitely calls for it.

"Go on in," Tellie says softly to the woman and sorta nudges her with his shoulder. She takes a tentative step and he says to her, "Biscuit's not gonna bite." Then louder to me: "You're not gonna bite her, are you, Biscuit?"

"No sir!" I say, a notch or two more cheerful than I actually feel. It's important to make the guards think you are all right even if your guts lay all over the floor next to you. "I gave up that bitin' a long time ago. Not good on the teeth and sometimes gives me the heartburn!"

He chuckles. "That's good, that's good." He says this almost to himself as if commenting on the quality of my humor. "Well, you take care of this one. She's mighty fresh. Show her the ropes and keep her out of trouble."

"Oh, you can be sure I will, Mr. Tellie, sir," I say, "We'll have her shaped up in no time."

"You do that," he says, slamming the cell door so that it latches, the sound echoing down the hall. He turns and walks around the corner out of sight, the tap of his nightstick against cell bars slowly receding.

But his new partner, a small wiry man—barely more than a boy it seems—doesn't move off so quickly. I'd seen him around the last couple of days but still hadn't learned his name. He hangs back a moment, his attention riveted on me, mouth partly open, tongue slowly moving over his front teeth left to right and then back again, lips curled just enough to make me wonder if he's grinning or if it's my imagination. I know my imagination and I know it isn't running wild. Right then I fully realize this kid—this scamp—is trouble. And I also realize that I will need to do something about him. Very soon. I've killed before and under the right circumstances, I won't hesitate to do it again. But only as a last resort. I don't want to risk my sentence getting extended.

I'm supposed to get out in three months.

New Madrid's Fault

***

"I'm on the top bunk."

The frail creature standing just inside the cell barely moves her eyes off the dusty floor to glance at me. Then I watch her shuffle to the lower bunk and busy herself with making the bed. I turn away, giving her as much physical space as I can in the ten-foot, five-inch by seven-foot concrete block cell, hole number 1112, of the Farmington Correctional Center for Women, my residence for the past fifteen years. In case you're interested, that's 73.5 square feet, including bunk beds and a small desk. More so than the physical space, I need to give my new roommate some emotional space so she can start getting herself acclimated to her surroundings. It's always a jolt, especially if you're not used to it. And she didn't look used to it.

Each cell is built to hold four prisoners for a total capacity of 290. I can't imagine that. It's a tight squeeze with just one cellie, let alone three others. The current bed count is half the capacity, though we have been getting a few more inmates each passing year.

Luckily, unlike male prisons, bathroom facilities are all centralized. The engineers who designed the joint must've thought it was too barbaric for females—even if they were prisoners—to be forced to sit and defecate in front of other women.

The showers are even separated by white curtains.

It's really not a bad joint, as far as prisons go, I suppose. Course I don't have anything to compare it to. This is the only one I've ever been in. But from what some of the other girls have said—either from personal experience, boyfriends, or brothers who've been in trouble with the Law—it's all right.

The prison is what's known as a medium-security facility, meaning we only get C-3 offenders or below: first-timers, drug users, thieves, murderers, of which I am a perfect fit. Bad enough, but none of the really hard cases or repeat offenders who are seen to be beyond rehabilitation. They still have hope for us, providing jobs, schooling, and any psych help we might need. I had just finished high school when I got here, but have since learned the ins and outs of bookkeeping and the fine art of doing laundry for over a hundred people. I figure that once I get out, I'll be perfectly suited for an accountant position at a chain of laundry mats.

"What's your name?"

New Madrid's Fault

"Sally." She sniffs. "Sally Caruthers."

"My name's Biscuit." I decide to keep my real name to myself for now. The fewer people who know it in here, the better, especially if I'm not sure I can trust them. Not that knowing my name is any big deal. But it is the one aspect of myself in prison that I can hold onto and keep hidden. It feels...I don't know...intimate or something. I'm careful who I give it out to.

My folks named me Francis Gardner but while my Mom was pregnant with me, all she craved were hot rolls. Since you can't very well call a little kid "Hot Roll" without someone giving you a funny look, I was stuck with "Biscuit." And now the family legend states pretty clearly that for my first five years, all I ate was hot biscuits smothered in butter. I can almost smell them right now, course I haven't had one ever since I landed behind bars.

My dad was the first to call me Biscuit when I was less than a year old. That was when life for my family was happy, with me sitting predominantly in the crosshairs of my father's affection. It soon changed, but back then, laughter flowed as deep as the alcohol did in years to come.

That was even when Richie was still alive.

"So, Miss Sally," I say, in my best I've-been-here-so-long-I'm-an-expert-on-everything voice, "let me tell you how it is around here. We wake up when Tellie starts banging his stick against the cells—" Sally quickly glances at me and then just as fast drops her eyes. "—and by 'stick,' I mean his club. We go to breakfast and if it's Monday, Wednesday, or Friday, I go down to the basement where I work in one of three crews that wash, dries, and folds the laundry for this entire correctional facility that you now call home. You'll be getting some kind of job soon. If it's not one of those days, I spend the rest of the morning in my cell when you might be getting your schooling or job training, if you need that. Then it's lunchtime, followed by an hour at the library or exercise outside. Then back to the cell. Maybe a nap, maybe reading. Supper's after that, along with showers three times a week. Back to the cell. Lights out. Next day, do it all over again. All in all, it's about sixteen hours a day in our cell. Stay out of my way and I'll stay out of yours."

Don't get me wrong. Maybe I sound cruel or bitter or that I'm whining. I'm not. I'm here because I deserve to be here. I have no one to blame but myself. It's just that some days are easier than others.

Sally turns her back on me and puts the final touches on the neatest, straightest, best-made bed I've ever seen. She tugs at the

New Madrid's Fault

gray blanket, completely erasing any hints of wrinkles in its fabric. I swivel in my chair, look at the paragraph I had written in my notebook, and sigh. I pick up the pencil again, hoping the words will start flowing but all I can concentrate on is Sally's movement behind me.

I reread my opening sentences and hate them. They're juvenile and amateurish. I am clearly not a writer but as I've gotten older and spent so much of my life in these 73.5 square feet confines and am faced with being released in a few short weeks, my desire for people—who I'm referring to will become painfully obvious—to understand the death and turmoil that put me here only grows stronger, like a bad case of the flu you can't shake. Truth has been distorted and even falsified. People can believe what they want to, but I at least want to give them the option of seeing what's real. So I've decided to write, to tell my story, my entire story, all of it. Yet I am terrified.

I pick up the green plastic sharpener and whittle away at my pencil, the unnecessary activity somehow comforting. One long, thin, wood shaving falls silently onto my desk like a tapeworm coughed up by a dog. Am I really sure I want to get into the whole mess again, to relive it all, to open the floodgates so to speak, to wallow for a while in the convoluted mess that was, and even more so became, my family, to be consumed with studying the evilness that took my innocence and stare at the bloody violence that forever marred me?

I've spent the better part of the last fifteen years trying to wash away the summer of 1953 with time and distance. I think the idea has always been that I could somehow separate myself from what happened so completely that I would become someone new, someone reborn, with no past and no history. That part of me simply would not exist anymore.

But denial can only take you so far and as hard as I've tried, I've never been able to completely forget. I remember everything: the smells, the fear, the pain, the weather, the exact spot in the book I had been reading, the sound of a body landing on the floor, the slight nuances and shifts in the atmosphere around me. Everything. Not a detail dulled as I had so desperately hoped.

The plastic sharpener stares at me out of its single black hole, a frozen, straight-line grin with only one razor blade tooth spread across its face. A small book sits to the right, my only possession in the world that I truly care about. It's thick—about two inches—yet only about five inches tall. It looks wrongly proportioned.

New Madrid's Fault

The book's cover is thick leather from the hide of a black bear, according to what's written inside. Its pages are old and yellow, able to be ground to a fine dust simply by turning a page in the wrong way. But its contents are as much a part of my history as they are a part of my future. That's really where my story must begin because everything is all connected in an inseparable blur.

I sigh again. The words won't come. I'm too distracted or have lost the inspiration or whatever it is writers need to write. I turn back to Sally. She continues smoothing out her blanket, rubbing her hands over and over the same section and I fear she's gonna put a hole in the thin material.

"So where you from?" I ask.

"Farmington." She stops her movement and straightens up. She's not sure what to do with her hands so she starts picking at a finger.

"Local girl, huh?" I say. "I guess I always figured they'd ship you off somewhere far away."

She answers with a shrug.

Farmington is a medium-sized farm town in lower Missouri about two hours west of where I grew up in "the bootheel." It's called that because...well, I hope you can figure that one out on your own. Anyway, I don't know much about the town except what I have read in the newspaper. I only ever saw it when I was brought here. Back when I was eighteen. Back when I was young.

It had been a cold, slimy November day, the kind that I have somehow always loved. The roads were slick with moisture from rain or fog or drizzle or something. I sat alone in the backseat of an unmarked police transport as it took me from the county jail to my new home. The facility was on the outskirts of town so I was able to see a few buildings—an Episcopal church with a high steeple, a small diner, a feed store, a handful of widely scattered homes—and trees. Lots of trees. Like I said, Farmington is in the middle of nowhere.

With good reason. Along with the correctional facility, Farmington is also home to one of the state's three mental hospitals. A crazy house. Whichever you prefer. Growing up, the best playground taunt always seemed to somehow culminate with a sort of variance along the theme of, "Oh yeah? Well, why don't you go back to your house—in Farmington!" You couldn't lose with a line like that.

New Madrid's Fault

However, on that chilly November afternoon, I realized that not only had I lost, but the game was over. That was when I realized that the women's correctional facility was right next door to the insane asylum. Some brilliant politician, I'm sure, woke up in the middle of the night with a surefire way to get reelected: "Eureka! Let's put all our social rejects in one, centralized location so they won't be spread out all over the place and destroy our peaceful lives by reminding us they exist!" I also discovered that law enforcement officers have their own unique brand of playground taunts. As we passed through the barbed fence approaching the twin concrete slabs in the distance—the correctional facility on the left, the insane asylum on the right—the officer in the passenger seat turned around to me with a greasy grin on his face and asked, "Would you prefer with or without nuts?" And then he and his partner burst into laughter.

It was a riot, let me tell you. Has been ever since.

Sally finally plops down on her bed but she immediately starts fiddling with it again, making sure the sheet and blanket are perfectly aligned. I figure her busyness has less to do with neatness and more to do with being nervous around me. I suddenly feel bad about how I acted toward her before.

I take a good look at her. She has dirty brown hair that partially blocks her face, but I can still see a blue smudge around her eye that I hadn't noticed before. I scoot my chair closer and reach out, my fingertips grazing her arm. She jerks back as if I'm a branding iron. I throw my hands up and sit back in my chair. "Okay, okay. I'm sorry."

Sally sniffs and wipes her eyes, the bruise even more apparent.

"You married?" I ask.

She nods, then quickly stops and shakes her head no.

"Were you married?"

She nods again.

"Divorced?"

No.

"Dead?"

New Madrid's Fault

Yes.

"He beat you?"

Yes.

"You kill him?"

A pause. Then yes. She wipes at her nose and says, "He had it coming."

"We all have it coming," I say.

Then she breaks down and cries.

Most recently, Stacey was a finalist in the Bardsy 2023 Summer First Chapter contest. In addition, he has had articles and study guides published online and in print, including numerous film reviews. His background in film and television production has only deepened his lifelong love of stories of all kinds. When not writing, he can be found playing pickleball (which he is obsessed with!) or in the kitchen working on a new recipe. He and his wife have replaced all three of their adult children (who have thankfully left the house) with three equally amazing dogs who are completely adorable. He has pics to prove that.

New Madrid's Fault

BETTER OFF DEAD

By Chloe McBride

Just do it, Kitty Dwyer thought to herself. *It's time to break up with him.*

Kitty peeked across the booth at her boyfriend, Lloyd Foley. He was hunched over the tabletop, fiddling absently with the tiny jukebox beside the salt shaker. Lloyd paged through the titles, more preoccupied with the click of the buttons than the selection of tracks. Kitty knew that he had no intention of choosing a new tune; he simply needed something to fixate on, a mindless task to create the illusion of presence. Lately, Kitty had found herself unsettled by Lloyd's vacant, maladaptive behavior. It was something about his eyes. They were like two crystal orbs, eerily luminous and swimming with indecipherable dreams. Their precise hue was unlike anything she had ever seen. They were a hypnotic shade of

Better Off Dead

silver, like the color of moonlight on snow. The color of loneliness.

"How was your sandwich?" Kitty asked, attempting conversation.

Lloyd didn't respond.

"*Lloyd*," Kitty said, raising her voice over the croon of Dion & The Belmonts.

This time, he heard her. "Huh?"

"I asked how your sandwich was."

"Oh." Lloyd's eyes returned to the jukebox. "It was good. Did you like your chocolate malt?"

Kitty forced a smile. "Yeah, I did. Thanks again."

A grin twitched across Lloyd's lips. He sank backwards and shifted his gaze to the window. Kitty wondered what Lloyd was thinking about. This was the thing she found so unsettling—the not knowing. Despite the frosty clearness of his eyes, Lloyd was an utterly unreadable person.

"Ready to go?" Lloyd asked, tossing a crumpled bill and a handful of coins onto the table.

"Mm-hmm." Kitty felt nauseated as she slid out of her seat. She walked quickly through the crowded diner, gulping in the greasy air. *What are you waiting for?!* she thought to herself.

"Could you walk on my right?" Lloyd asked, side-stepping Kitty as they ambled down the sidewalk. He gently extracted the pile of textbooks from her hands and tucked them beneath his arm.

"Uh-sorry," Kitty mumbled, pulling her spool of long, raven hair over her shoulder. "I forgot."

Lloyd had been deaf in his left ear since his premature birth--a disability made worse by his mother's habit of cleaning her children's waxy ears with safety pins. In addition to his impaired hearing, Lloyd *was* one of the scrawnier, sallower boys in his class. He walked with a pigeon-toed gait and struggled with running or walking long distances. However, these things held no bearing on Kitty's love for Lloyd, or her loss of it. The only person who thought less of Lloyd was Lloyd.

"Want to stop at the record store?" Lloyd asked, scratching his

Better Off Dead

blonde crew cut. "I know you've had your eye on *Between the Buttons*."

"No, thank you," Kitty lied. "Can we just walk back to your house?"

Lloyd nodded and stuffed his free hand into the pockets of his gray uniform slacks. As was typical of the teenagers who lived in Tacwood, Pennsylvania, Lloyd attended Holy Castle, an all-boys Catholic high school. It was easy to spot Castle students on the street; their required dress was a powder-blue Oxford shirt with a red sweater vest on top. Kitty went to Bishop of Athens, the all-girls partner school across the street from Lloyd's. They took classes in separate buildings, but melded together for Mass on Wednesdays and Fridays. In contrast to the boys, Athens girls wore brown jumpers with yellow Oxfords and brown knee socks. "Troop 666" had become their infamous nickname.

It was common, almost understood, that Castle boys dated Athens girls. In an act of well-intended pity, Lloyd and Kitty's already-coupled friends had set them up on a blind date six months prior. She reluctantly accepted in the hopes of capturing the envy of her preferred choice, Bruce Peterson. Much to Kitty's dismay, her relationship with Lloyd hadn't caused so much as a ripple of awareness in Bruce's life. This forced Kitty to reconsider her

Bardsy 2023 Fall Anthology — First Chapters

strategy, to break up with the kind, cowardly boy who hadn't done a single thing wrong.

Lloyd was a good person, passive to a fault, so it hurt Kitty to know how easily he'd accept her decision. She could clearly imagine the way his rain cloud eyes would widen at the sting of her words, but he'd accept those words nonetheless. He'd respect her decision and nod politely. He'd wish her well and sulk away to lick his wounds in silence. He wouldn't pine or pester. Lloyd would leave her alone.

"Do you want to hang out some more?" Lloyd asked as they reached the top of his street. "Or would you like me to take you home?"

"Home is fine," said Kitty. She'd take the weekend to think things over.

They walked side-by-side down the block, which was flanked on both sides by ramshackle row homes, mile-high lawns, and ornamental Catholic statues. Kitty watched her saddle shoes drag along the macadam, avoiding the holy scrutiny of St. Michael, St. Gabriel, and two dozen Mary Magdalenes. From end to end, the street was a jovial blur of baseball mitts and bicycle bells. It was late spring, but the stirrings of summer were spilling into its preceding season. Evenings were longer, lighter, illuminated by

Better Off Dead

sherbert light and fireflies. Neighbors grilled on patios and toasted cheap sixers over chain-linked fences. The air was a warm perfume of cigarettes, charred chicken, and sweet, buttered corn. Kitty felt mocked by the happiness around her.

"Let me grab my keys," Lloyd said as they reached his front door. Quizzically he glanced around the front lawn.

"What's the matter?" Kitty asked.

"None of the kids are outside." He took one last look at Kitty before disappearing behind the tattered screen door.

Kitty found this odd, too. Lloyd was the oldest of ten siblings, all of whom were usually running down the sidewalks or spilling from the windows. The couple spent most of their time at Lloyd's house, but this was the first time she'd ever seen it so tranquil. Kitty was surprised to find herself missing the madness. As the only child in a cold and loveless household, Kitty had become fond of the Foley family's chaotic dynamic, of their loud and unconditional adoration for each other. It was one of the things that made the breakup with Lloyd that much harder--losing him meant losing his family, too. The idea of being alone curdled her stomach, but returning to the company of her uptight family was enough to

Bardsy 2023 Fall Anthology — First Chapters

upheave her chocolate malt.

As Kitty idled beneath the torn porch awning, she wondered what her parents would make of her breaking up with Lloyd. He was the only boyfriend she'd ever introduced to them. The Dwyers didn't particularly *like* Lloyd--then again, they didn't like much of anything. But they tolerated his quiet, non-threatening demeanor. Mr. and Mrs. Dwyer knew that there would be no nonsense, no *funny business*, while their daughter was with a guy like Lloyd. Most teenage couples couldn't keep their hands off of each other. On the contrary, Kitty and Lloyd barely even *held* hands. That was the way it should be, according to the Dwyers. Life was not supposed to be a passionate affair. It was about surviving, acquiring, and dying.

While Kitty considered the potential receptions to her decision, the screen door burst open behind her. Lloyd was frozen on the porch, his face bewildered and green.

"Are you okay?" Kitty cried, widening her deep, blue eyes.

"No," he breathed. "Something's wrong with Abigail."

Kitty understood immediately. Abigail Foley, the youngest of Lloyd's

Better Off Dead

many siblings, had been hanging on the cusp of death since birth. Abigail was a polio survivor, but the illness had left her paralyzed on the right side of her body. The Foleys could not afford the medical upkeep of their many children; at least half of them were in need of things like glasses, braces, and in Lloyd's case, hearing aids. However, Abigail's issues were the most demanding, which forced the family to de-prioritize their lesser needs.

Abigail was home-schooled and kept indoors most of the time. Sometimes, Mrs. Foley would let Lloyd and Kitty take Abigail on walks--*practice for the future,* she often teased. Per Abigail's request, the two of them placed her tiny body in a red wagon and pulled her through the neighborhood. Abigail would lay back in the clunking carriage, watching in silence as sunlight flickered through the passing tree branches.

Kitty had come to love Lloyd's sickly sister. She had a way of softening her big brother, of bringing forth a joy that Kitty herself couldn't draw out of him. Whenever the couple looked after Abigail, Lloyd was talkative. Funny, even. Lloyd and Kitty watched Abigail so frequently that she really did feel something like a test-run child. This surrogate parenting gave Kitty hope for the future. Perhaps Lloyd's shortcomings as a partner would be balanced by his attentiveness as a father. If Kitty could just hold out for a few more years and catch up to the sense of responsibility that Lloyd already possessed, then maybe she could really love him.

Maybe.

"What's wrong with her?" Kitty demanded, following Lloyd into the house. The other eight Foley kids were already gathered in the living room, a gangle of underfed limbs cradling each other on the mismatched furniture. From the second floor, Mrs. Foley's anguished wails shook the house like a reckoning.

Lloyd looked around at his helpless brothers and sisters, suddenly harnessing an uncharacteristic sense of calm. He settled the children, then flew up the stairs to assist his mother. Kitty waited on the sofa. Two of Lloyd's young sisters huddled up next to her, and she stroked their hair while they cried.

"A-abby is s-sick," whimpered Ellie, a freckle-faced ten-year-old. Her eyes, the same spectral silver as Lloyd's, were crimson and swollen around the lids.

"Sick how?" Kitty asked quietly.

Ellie shrugged. "Mommy said her fever's real high."

Better Off Dead

Before Kitty could make sense of this, footsteps thundered down the stairs. Lloyd had his strawberry-haired sister swaddled in a bedsheet. She was conscious but limp. Blood hemorrhaged from her nose, her mouth, her ears, her backside. Ellie gasped at the sight of the stained fabric.

"We're going to the hospital," Lloyd explained urgently. Presently, he was the only member of the family with enough composure to operate a vehicle. His parents hurried behind him and dashed to the car.

"Can you stay with the kids?" he asked.

Kitty stared fearfully at him. "Y-yes," she said. But Lloyd was gone before she answered.

After the car peeled away, Kitty left word with her parents. She put on the television for the children and prepared a heap of spaghetti that went untouched. As dusk phased to dark, the children scattered around the living room and drifted to sleep one by one. It was tragic, the way the Foley siblings could sleep so soundly on the floor without pillows or blankets. George and Bill, twin brothers closest in age to Lloyd, stayed awake with Kitty.

"Sure was nice of you to stick around," George mumbled shortly after midnight. "I know it means a lot to Lloyd."

Kitty blushed. "Thanks, George. Bill, you hanging in there?"

Bill, who was dozing at the kitchen table, raised his head from the crook of his arm. "I guess so," he mumbled.

Kitty didn't push. Bill spoke so seldomly that he made Lloyd seem verbose.

"He loves you, you know," George said quietly.

Kitty smirked. "Who, Bill? No kidding."

George chuckled. At the table, Bill smiled with his eyes closed.

"Don't tell Lloyd I said so," George added. "I just thought you should know since that dumbass won't say it himself."

"It's alright," Kitty insisted. Suddenly, her heart began to swell--not with love, but with guilt. How could she possibly break up with Lloyd? How utterly selfish was she to even think of her own feelings

Better Off Dead

at such a time? This day, whatever the outcome, would bond them forever. Even if Kitty ended things with Lloyd, she would remain etched into this catastrophe. A thumb on the lens of the memory.

Was this fate? Was this God's path for her? During Mass, she'd prayed for the man of her dreams, but even God knew that Jim Morrison wasn't going to answer those love letters. Was Lloyd *Foley* really her forever? Kitty sat back and concentrated, waiting for the realization of their love to wash over her. She waited until Bill was snoring in the kitchen. She waited until George retreated upstairs to sleep in an open bed. She waited until night phased to dawn. The feeling never came.

Kitty knew that she admired Lloyd, but she didn't love him. She also knew that she couldn't bring herself to tell him. Not now. Maybe not ever.

She was asleep when Lloyd finally returned home. Kitty's eyes fluttered open as Lloyd entered the house. He was alone. Mr. and Mrs. Foley were still in the car, both inconsolable. Balled in Lloyd's grasp was the blood-stained bedsheet.

For an eternal moment, Kitty and Lloyd stared at each other over the sea of his snoring siblings, their breath rising and falling in calm waves. They continued to sleep without disruption, blissfully unaware of the news they'd soon wake up to.

***

The day that followed was like being in Hell. Kitty had never heard so many people cry so hard at once. She stayed well into the afternoon, cooking, cleaning, consoling. By dinnertime, Kitty was on the brink of exhaustion. She sat beside Lloyd on the couch, resting her head on his shoulder. Both of them were still wearing their school uniforms. The blue sleeves of Lloyd's shirt were stained with Abigail's blood.

"You can get going if you need to," Lloyd said. "Really, it's fine. You've been so helpful."

Kitty looked up at him. "Are you sure?" she asked. "I'll come right back. I just need to close my eyes for a few minutes and get changed."

Lloyd smirked and sniffed her. "You could use a shower, too."

A woeful grin tugged at the corners of Kitty's mouth. "I mean it, Lloyd. Will you be okay for a little while?"

"I will," Lloyd assured her. "Want me to take you home?"

"That's okay," she said. "Be with your family. Could I use the phone to call home?"

Lloyd walked Kitty to the mailbox. The street was full of life, just as it had been the day before, but a subtle hush had fallen over the onlookers. Neighbors craned their necks at Lloyd and Kitty, hungry for crumbs of information. The couple stood facing each other, a sidewalk's width of distance between them. To Kitty's surprise, Lloyd's gaze was not off in some faraway place. He was staring right at her, his gray eyes boring into her blue ones. An iceberg in an ocean.

"This doesn't feel real," Lloyd said.

Kitty touched his cheek. "I know."

She dropped her hand as her father's car turned around the corner. Mr. Dwyer crept down the street, waving curtly at the neighbors. He cut the engine and climbed out of the car.

"Hello, Lloyd," said Mr. Dwyer, his voice dispassionate as he extended a stiff hand. "I'm very sorry for your loss."

Lloyd accepted the gesture. "Thank you, sir."

Mr. Dwyer tipped his hat. "Please extend my condolences to your folks. Kathleen, are you ready to go home?"

"Yes." She glanced at Lloyd and flashed him a weak smile. "I'll call you later, alright?"

Lloyd nodded and shuffled back inside.

The drive home was strange and tense. Kitty wasn't often alone with her father, and she could tell that the interaction was making him uneasy. Mr. Dwyer was a mean, rigid man whose only traceable emotion was an ever-shifting spectrum of anger.

"Jesus, Mary, and Joseph," Mr. Dwyer muttered, glaring through the windshield at the houses on Lloyd's street. "Would it kill these bums to mow their goddamn lawns?"

Kitty stayed quiet. Her father's disdainful rants were always rhetorical, and ended quicker when he remained unchallenged.

"Did they say what killed her?" Mr. Dwyer asked.

At the sound of the question, Kitty felt the floor bottom out beneath her. It was a sentiment she hadn't yet processed. In those long hours of comforting Lloyd's family, nobody had actually spoken the truth out loud: Abigail was dead.

"No," Kitty mumbled, hot tears pooling in her eyes. "I felt, you know… it would be *rude* to ask."

Mr. Dwyer nodded. "I'm sure we'll find out soon enough. No matter the reason, this was probably for the best."

Kitty blinked at her father, gut-punched by his words. "How do you mean?"

"That little girl was suffering," Mr. Dwyer replied without missing a beat. "She couldn't walk. She couldn't attend school. She couldn't even use the bathroom by herself. Think about that, Kathleen. Would you want that life? A sick, shortened life of constant pain?"

Kitty thought about this for a long moment. "I don't know, Dad. Abigail seemed happy to me."

"She knew no other happiness," said her father. "You will not understand this until you're a parent, Kathleen, but that child is better off dead."

Chloe McBride was born in Philadelphia, Pennsylvania. In 2018, she earned her bachelor's degree from Kutztown University with a focus on clinical psychology. She currently works in the field of early childhood education, but her primary ambition is to become a professional author. McBride spends the majority of her free time in front of a keyboard with a pair of headphones permanently attached to her ears. Presently, she resides in North Carolina.

THE LUCK OF SAINTS

By Kate Altman

Moving in the shadows of San Giovanni, I stared down the empty street and got my second glimpse of the Alleyway of Death. The bishop and I were swathed in black robes, allowing the church's darkness to swallow our forms. The evening was warm for March, but the mist that rolled off the water wasn't the only thing that made me shiver as we moved towards the narrow brick corridor.

The time had once again come for Saint Mark to spill blood into the canals of Venice. I could practically feel him walking behind us, almost hear his whisper in the breeze. *"It is for La Serenissima,"* he would say, *"Be grateful."* He would look like he did in my dreams: a pale porcelain mask for a face, empty eyes, a black velvet duster, and a ridiculous-looking tricorn hat.

The Luck Of Saints

I collided with a heavy wall of fabric, and was ripped from my imagination when I nearly tumbled sideways into the dirty water.

"Pay attention, Senka." Bishop Rossi hissed.

"I *am* paying attention," I grumbled, "But I can hardly see in this thing." I pushed at the raggedy fabric of my oversized hood. "I don't understand why we have to dress like dirty old hags." The irritation that flitted across his wrinkled face didn't surprise me. The elders didn't like me on principle–especially Bishop Rossi. They didn't think that little girls with sharp tongues made ideal *novizi*.

"These cloaks are laced with blessings by the saints themselves," he scoffed, sticking his lumpy nose into the air. "It is an honor to wear them."

Any kind of clever retort slipped away. *An honor.* The words burned in my throat like bad liquor. There was no honor in what would happen tonight.

Bishop Rossi began walking again, his cloak hissing against the cobblestone as he moved down a narrow passageway and into a small empty plaza. It had one entrance and one exit, and a small pile of garbage rested in the corner. At its center was a cracked white fountain, darkly stained with water that was long gone. This was the edge of Santa Croce, the oldest district closest to the ports that reeked with fish and ran rampant with crime.

It was the perfect place to commit a murder.

Somewhere down the streets, someone was laughing–probably a drunk based on the way his words slurred between chuckles. *Someone is laughing, and someone else is about to die.* I could feel death prickle in the air, sharp and numbing against my cheeks. Glancing at the dark corridor directly ahead, I suppressed a shudder. I'd seen the *Calle de la Morte* once before when I was drawn to it as a young girl. On the streets, I'd heard the stories of a place where the Council of Ten lured Venice's enemies for assassination. It had seemed bigger then, more menacing and full of evil. That night, its depth had seemed endless. Now, in the purple twilight that cast long shadows across its ancient stones, it was almost beautiful.

The toll of a clock tower sounded, and I tore my attention from the dichotomous lane. Seven chimes.

"You are simply an observer," Bishop Rossi ordered, turning to me. "You will stay here and keep the watch. Have you prepared yourself

The Luck Of Saints

adequately this time?"

"Yes, *signore*." I said, fighting the urge to spit the words at him. "But I am also no longer a little girl." In preparation, I'd skipped dinner–which was something street rats tended to do anyway. The last time I'd witnessed the sword of Saint Mark in action, I'd spewed what little I'd had in my stomach into the canal. But I was stronger now. I had to be.

"Yes, well, I know that your talents can cause you… weakness," he said, studying me. "But within The Head, such weaknesses are unacceptable."

"It won't be a problem." I insisted. I was well aware of just how unacceptable he found me, despite the talents that made me invaluable.

The Bishop pushed back his hood and reached into the depths of his cloak. In its tattered leather scabbard, which was as ancient as the saints themselves, the sword of Saint Mark didn't look like much. But I knew better. With a gentle hiss, he pulled it free and into the fading light. It was simple, but unarguably beautiful, made of ornately carved silver that bled into the long dark blade that ended at a lethal point.

"Take your watch, Senka," Bishop Rossi commanded. "And fulfill your duty." With a flourish of his cloak, he walked into the alleyway and disappeared into its blackness.

Despite everything, I almost laughed. *Who said old men couldn't have a flair for the dramatic?*

Pushing back my hood, I moved to the fountain and ran my hand along the inside of its reservoir. Dusty traces of grime accumulated on my palm and I smeared the filth across my face. I grabbed a cracked tin from the garbage and sat hard on the ground. The ratty cloak would've been enough, but the dirt and begging could really sell it.

No one liked to look at sad, filthy street-rats, especially the young ones. I'd had years of experience being invisible. I might as well use them to my advantage.

Leaning into the hard fountain walls, my back to the dead-end alley, I began to wait. I watched the street through the narrow passageway through which we had come. Night time was falling, and the floating city was about to come to life.

At first, it was just one person, an old woman that moved

strenuously down the street. But when the streetlamps flickered on, the people began to come; called to the city's heart for all its enticing sins. It wasn't called *La Serenissima* for nothing. Venice was the shining republic of the Adriatic Sea. Tourists, merchants, artists, and bankers, traveled here alike to experience the endless grandeur and scandalous nightlife. Gambling away life savings or drinking yourself half to death was just part of the charm, one that I'd seen worked once before, and with *Carnevale* right around the corner, the number of desperate souls would double.

There was a part of me that despised the people who came here to lose themselves. They couldn't see a good thing when they had it. But when the vices were wrapped up like enticing presents, watching exquisite freedom and expression bloom became addicting.

As darkness fell, it became difficult to know who to look for. Flocks of people in feathers and rags and suits choked the street. When I was young, I liked to make up stories about them; to speculate wildly about the details of their lives. Like the beautiful woman in black skirts and a lace veil who applied red lipstick into the streetlight, perhaps she was on her way to meet a forbidden lover. Maybe the laughing elderly couple had twenty grandchildren back home in France. Perhaps the young man selling papers, who stole pocket watches and wallets with slick fingers, was training to be a magician. I had to force myself to stop. Wondering about people would only further the tragedy when one of them was about to die. I began counting as a distraction.

At four hundred and twelve, a man stopped. He was young, probably not much older than I was, but his appearance was worlds away. He was beautiful in a terrible kind of way; all sharp angles and dark features that looked like they enjoyed playing cruel tricks. He stood out from the crowd, didn't laugh or rush as he reached into his dark tailored coat, pulled out a lighter, and lit a cigarette.

Was this him? Was this who Bishop Rossi waited for? I could usually sense these sorts of things, but perhaps I was too far away to pick anything up. As if feeling my gaze, he looked up, and keen eyes met my own as he let out a puff of smoke. I held his stare. He would look away–they all did, eventually.

But he didn't.

He took the cigarette between his fingers, a line of smoke drifting into the air, and just kept staring. It was honestly starting to get rather creepy, and in an act of defiance, I raised an eyebrow at him and deepened my scowl before pulling the hood farther over my

The Luck Of Saints

face.

He grinned.

He actually *grinned*, and though I was too far away to be certain, I could've sworn he winked before dissolving back into the crowd. I didn't have time to dissect the strange interaction, because just as soon as the beautiful boy in the dark coat disappeared, the man we had been waiting for arrived.

He was middle-aged, not too tall, with a receding hairline, sharp chin, and beady eyes that darted back and forth. The moment he appeared, I knew it was him. I could smell it on his skin. Death, like iron and rot and something meant to be buried. Faint shadows trailed from his figure, obscuring it, like he was already becoming a ghost.

He reached into his brown overcoat and pulled out a flat leather folder.

Letting out a low-toned whistle, I nestled deeper into my cloak and sunk lazily into the hard ground. I watched him squeeze through the narrow entrance to the plaza, eyeing me nervously, but the minute I pushed my rusted cup in his direction, he averted his gaze.

"I don't have any coin for you, girl." He grumbled and kicked my empty cup, snaking his way around the fountain to seal his fate.

This is wrong, I thought, and I nearly reached out a hand to stop him.

But I didn't.

Perhaps it was because I was selfish, because I knew it would cost me everything I'd worked for. But I knew this wasn't true. Instead, I did nothing for the worst reason; because I was afraid.

As the man vanished into the shadows, I could see the ghostly form of Saint Mark in his wake. His *volto* mask and high-collared coat materialized from my nightmares as he waited for his will to be enacted.

I didn't need to be watching to know when it happened. Goosebumps had pebbled my arms. I'd sensed the shift in the air, and felt the rush of life rise and cease. Then, the silhouette of Saint Mark had strolled from the gloomy lane and disappeared into the fog.

The deed had been done.

The Luck Of Saints

Bishop Rossi emerged a moment later. He looked exactly the same. No blood, no wounds, nothing. It hadn't felt violent, but I'd somehow expected him to look different. But he only stared at me with his same disapproving expression, utterly unfazed.

"You did well." He admitted, though the sternness of his tone did nothing to aid the words. "Did your... *talento* manifest as usual?" He spat the word *talent*, like the curse it was.

"I sensed death's mark on his skin, saw the aura it left, and felt the moment his life ended." I said the words dully and without feeling, like they didn't tear up my insides when I spoke them. "It was all the same." I decided to keep the masked figure I had seen to myself. It had taken the elders years to trust in my ability to sense death. Telling them that I had begun seeing dead saints was unlikely to instill confidence.

No one wanted spies or assassins that were on the edge of losing their minds

"Who was he?" I blurted.

Bishop Rossi's eyes could've sliced me open. We weren't supposed to ask questions. "A traitor. Someone who wanted to harm the serenity we've built." He said. With that, he slipped out of the plaza and into the street like nothing had even happened.

***

We began walking back to The Basilica of Saint Mark; to home, or at least the closest thing I had to one. Though night had heavily fallen, the city sang with life. Gondoliers bartered loudly with customers, performers drew crowds for coins, and the sounds of chaos bled into the street from taverns and saloons that threw light into the canals. Everything seemed to shine, even the stars.

I tried to enjoy it, to let the warmth of life wash away the guilt and terror that threatened to drown me. But the prickle of death persisted. It numbed my fingertips and pounded in my head like a drummer keeping a beat.

We crossed the bridge into the eastern districts, and Saint Mark's Square, dwarfed by the towering basilica, came into view. Despite the cold secrets I knew it held, St. Mark's Basilica had never failed to steal my breath. It shone with the wealth and power of Venice; its intricate carvings and golden domes erupted from the cobblestone square, reaching upwards like hands grasping for the heavens.

The Luck Of Saints

I stumbled, realizing that the pain in my head had grown steadily worse, and my boot tangled with a larger leg. I caught myself against the bridge's railing.

"Watch yourself!" shouted the man, then eyed my dirty face and rags. "Street-scum." he hissed.

I threw him a gesture that he didn't seem to like. "Piss off, you drunk bastard!" I yelled, but the words had no bite. My head was *screaming*. The lights swirled, and it wasn't until I saw the familiar white face that I realized this wasn't over. He stood motionless at the square's edge, staring at me with eyes that swallowed the night.

Then he was gone.

"Get up, Senka." Bishop Rossi growled, seizing my arm. "What is wrong with you, girl?"

I clutched at his shoulders, desperation and panic swelling in my chest. "This isn't over." I whispered urgently, my eyes wildly searching the crowd for shadows and stench. "Something is about to happen."

As if on cue, a scream pierced the night. I pushed away from Bishop

Rossi and threw myself towards the crowded square. Revelers and tourists shouted curses at me in languages I didn't know, but I didn't care. I just had to get there in time.

More screaming erupted from the square. I raced across the plaza to where a small crowd gathered at the basilica's edge. It was usually packed with musicians and dancers, but the square had been cleared to prepare for *Carnevale*. The city had begun to hang large swaths of colorful fabric from the buildings. The surrounding rooftops were adorned with strings of multicolored flags that swung between the narrow gaps.

I reached the crowd, my breathing ragged. A man was crying, someone else was shouting, but the rest of the observers were utterly frozen. At the edge of the pack, an elderly woman kneeled against the stone, praying and rocking as she clutched her necklace and murmured to herself.

I placed a gentle arm on her shoulder. "*Signora*, please, what has happened?"

She didn't look at me. Didn't say anything. She only pointed with a shaking gnarled hand into the darkness ahead, where a man in a bleached porcelain mask loomed before dissolving into the

The Luck Of Saints

shadows.

"Signora-" I began again, but stopped as I watched her finger slowly rise.

Following it, I looked up.

There, halfway up the ancient hewn passageway between two buildings, something was *hanging*. The form was nothing more than a silhouette in the gloom, but I could discern the string of colorful flags that wrapped around one leg and caused the rest of the limbs to splay out like a twisted star. Something glistening and dark dribbled down the wall and into a puddle on the ground.

I gaped, dread and despair bubbling into my throat. I had been too late.

A firm hand squeezed my shoulder, causing me to jump. Bishop Rossi. He surveyed the scene with world-ending wrath, the kind that would make me scurry into the corner if it was turned in my direction. Without a word, he withdrew the sword from his cloak and moved noiselessly into the passageway. He would be a hound hunting for blood, ready to dole out Saint Mark's vengeance as he saw fit.

Things were about to change. This was a blow that would stir The Head into a frenzy, struck right at the heart of our organization.

There was a body in the alleyway.

This was a problem, because we hadn't been the ones to put it there.

Kate is a recent college graduate with a bachelors degree in Art & Art History. She works as a content creator across multiple social media platforms making short artistic videos. She enjoys any form of artistic storytelling and is a painter, screen writer, and creative writer in her free-time.

The Luck Of Saints

THE SCORCHED SKY

By Erin Bashford

Something's outside.

It's not going to be a problem. Eiranth's protective spells will hold up. They need reigniting every few days, but she did it yesterday, so Eiranth shrugs and turns her attention back to her food. The swamp's humid air has already melted the ice in her cold noodle broth.

The sound comes again; a wet, grating scratch grumbles through the room. Eiranth places the bowl on the table and leans back to glance out of the kitchen window, careful not to move so much that her face is visible from outside. She holds her breath.

There's nothing there but the nighttime glow of firebugs and luminescent algae on the swamp's surface.

Zap your worrying trap, Eiranth tells herself. Last night she stayed at a client's house for a minute too long. She'd been too distracted by their display of laileve stones, embedded into their mortar walls like the swamp water's stars. It was rare that households with no zenites were allowed the stones, even to display. A mundane household, occupying an equally mundane home, in the mundane town of Silla's Glade, simply did not *have* iolites and gaspetites.

Eiranth pools broth onto her spoon. *Did they follow me? Did my laileves expire too soon?* Eiranth peers out of the kitchen window again, blood throbbing in her ears. The porch is empty, illuminated by the celestial algae. Only the murmur of crickets and firebugs trickles through the air.

Besides, even if anyone is daft enough to climb up seven electrified ladders to her treehouse, they will find nothing more than an abandoned shack. Eiranth's cloaking and protective spells will trick any intruder.

Eiranth slurps the ice broth before her stomach twinges and panic floods her mind.

Did I reignite the protective spells?

Last night her laileves expired before she left the client's house, but she wouldn't have forgotten the most important layer of protection. Would she? In seven years, she had never forgotten the cloaking spells. Her mother had taught her an impenetrable combination of laileves, and it had never failed. Mother had always told her to stay hidden.

But last night was different, wasn't it? Her magic had spluttered out, having spent too long enraptured by the client's collection. And she'd…

The food seemingly expands in her mouth, blocking her airways.

She had sprinted home and stumbled into bed, utterly exhausted by the night's labor.

With now warm noodles as heavy as swamp clay in her mouth, she freezes when the squelchy, groaning sounds come from her porch again.

She spits the food back into her bowl and launches herself into a stand. *Go, go, go.* She silently castigates herself as she taps the

The Scorched Sky

dermal laileve stones in her lower scalp. The back of her hair, from the tip of her ears to the nape of her neck, is shaved, with twelve crystals embedded into her skin. They've been there so long she doesn't feel them anymore. She taps them when she needs their strength. But even that's just a force of habit, a redundant comfort. All she needs to activate their magic is a thought.

Abandoning her bowl on the rickety table, she creeps to the front door. Before she can talk herself out of it, she yanks the door open and her stomach leaps into the swamp below.

A relieved grimace blooms on her face.

"Oh," Eiranth says. "It's just you."

On her doorstep lies Fugue, a grotesque green glob with whom she has had a long-standing disagreement. He squelches there, as dark green as the aventurine and serpentine laileves in her scalp. Unlike the stones, he's wet, slimy, inhuman, and somehow speaks.

"Two…" groans Fugue. How sound can come from his nonexistent mouth, Eiranth is unsure. Merely pondering his existence, with his formless glob-like shape and the guttural squelch that comes from his throat, is enough to send her into a craze.

"Get off my doorstep," Eiranth says, bringing her foot down to hover over Fugue's mucilaginous form. "You cantankerous glob."

Fugue, somehow, twists his head up to meet Eiranth's eyes. He doesn't have a head, but that's all Eiranth knows to compare it to. He doesn't have eyes, but there are two slightly darker calderas where his eyes would be. So, Eiranth inexplicably maintains eye contact with the eyeless creature, grinding her teeth as she does so. She hasn't considered how he is alive, how he is sentient, or why he believes he lives on her porch, because if she thinks about it for a second, perplexed nausea rises in her throat.

"Two…" Fugue repeats, his viscous body shuddering, almost like he's trying to grab her ankle.

Eiranth cocks her eyebrow. "Two *seconds* until I stamp on you so hard you'll be sent straight into the swamp."

"Two suns—"

Eiranth hovers her foot over his head. "Oh, zap your trap, you monster."

"Eye…" Fugue grumbles. It's what he calls her. *Eiranth* is too much

The Scorched Sky

for his nonexistent throat.

"What?" She kicks her foot closer to his body. "What do you want?"

"Friend…" Fugue squelches out from under Eiranth's foot and reshapes himself so he's almost flat.

Eiranth sighs. It has been a long time since they talked. "Fine." She nudges the door open. "Come in."

Fugue squelches over the threshold, his grotesque body slopping into her kitchen like… well, like algae slops across the swamp's surface. Eiranth clicks the door shut behind them. The kitchen seems darker, with shadows occupying the corners. The glowing swamp always tricks her eyes.

Fugue clambers up the chair with his nonexistent limbs. He stares at her, his blob eyes vacant, and stretches two elongated clumps of algae in front of him like arms. When he reaches the table, he peers into the soup bowl and rolls his head to face Eiranth.

"Not finish…." he groans, the sound like wet mud squeezed through fingers.

"No," Eiranth says, trying to keep up her facade of anger. "Because *you interrupted me.*"

Fugue twists his head around the room. "Messy."

How dare he intrude her peace to criticize her housekeeping habits? Eiranth glowers at him. "Because you interrupted me."

"Long time messy…" Fugue croaks.

"Get *out*," Eiranth says, striding across the small kitchen. She picks up her spoon and pokes Fugue with it. "You're a monster. You shouldn't exist. Go and prey on another unassuming innocent victim, you scourge." She sets her jaw and raises her upper lip into a snarl. "Get out."

Fugue cowers. He knows what will happen now. He will leave, but before the week ends, he will return. And Eiranth will let him in because she'll be happy to see him. If even to simply argue with him. Just something that responds, that she doesn't have to cloak herself to talk to, and that won't forget her as soon as she turns away.

Eiranth steps backwards, not tearing her eyes from Fugue's, and tugs the door open. "Out. Get."

Fugue lowers his head and flops from the table. He squelches towards the door, each small movement wet and gelatinous on the shimmering stone floor.

And then he's gone, and Eiranth shudders. One day, she will find whichever cursed part of the swamp birthed him and drain it dry.

Her skin simmers with rage. For once, it's not the humidity of summer melting her skin, but undiluted fury. She grounds herself through the shimmering floor; it cools her from the bottom up, settling her anger. Even at night, the shards of opalescent stone immersed in her kitchen floor glimmer. It's her favorite thing about the house. That, and that it's so far up a ladder system that no one can be bothered to climb up. Except Fugue.

Eiranth abandons her meal on the table, given it was touched by a congealed glob monster, and pulls a dried strawberry and cricket skewer from her snack cupboard. She needs to get out of the house. The place doesn't feel... right. Whether that's due to Fugue's interruption or something else, she is unsure.

She follows Fugue's path onto the veranda. It's hotter outside, and sweat pricks across her forehead. Crawling green vines hang from the cypress' lowest branches, tickling her hair as she takes her seat on the porch chair. She leans against the veranda railings, the frustration of her encounter with Fugue bubbling only in her stomach. For Eiranth, hunger-influenced rage is not unprecedented. She makes eye contact with the first impaled cricket. "You're the lucky one," she says to it before shoving it into her mouth. As her jaws work, her laileves tingle.

"Probably need cleaning," she mutters, crunching the insect in her mouth. Almost ironically, the night is alive with the sound of crickets. She imagines their little legs rubbing together, singing on the tree branches, their soundless cousins the firebugs glowing high in the night's sky.

Eiranth follows a particularly energetic firebug with her eyes; it spirals into the sky, darting behind a thicket of leaves. She relaxes into the chair. Tonight, the night sky is empty. Summer nights in Silla's Glade are rarely clear. Has she even seen the sun this week? She knows Ausola must be there, hiding behind the clouds, because her laileves function. If Ausola's sun died again, her magic would forever be uncharged.

Besides, Eiranth thinks with distaste, *I usually wake up in the*

The Scorched Sky

afternoon. Then, there's never much sun left to catch a glimpse of.

"I should be worried," she whispers to herself. "If I don't see her, does she even exist? What if she's left us again?"

As if answering her question, a flash bursts behind her. Eiranth jumps from the chair and her heart races. *What in Ausola…?* One of her laileves pricks under her skin—the aventurine. She nites it and the leaves around her come alive, every dust particle shimmers in the air, each swamp creature's movement flickering in her vision. She drops to a crouch and creeps to her door.

Without moving, nites the jasper embedded parallel to her left ear. Her hearing purifies; the nighttime ambience fades, crickets and her racing heart silence. Eiranth angles her hearing inside her kitchen. *The fucking cloaking spells,* she realizes with heavy dread. She didn't finish.

That doesn't explain the flash, though. Expired cloaking spells have never created light before. In a town that craves light, they would have figured out a way by now. The night would never be dark.

In her kitchen, a throat is cleared. Another sprinting heart thrumming away, rattling inside a ribcage. Panicked, rapid breathing.

It's just Fugue, she attempts to persuade herself, but even she doesn't believe her thoughts. Eiranth knows Fugue does not breathe, he does not have a heart, or a throat. Eiranth pulls a steady breath into her chest.

Before she can scare herself, she yanks the kitchen door open.

There is no Fugue in her low-ceilinged kitchen. The kitchen is empty, and her discarded food is still on the table.

Only two other rooms; the living room and her bedroom. She crosses her kitchen on all fours, ensuring her limbs touch the stone floor softly. No obvious weapons are within easy reach. There's a spoon, a wooden board, and a--a two-pronged fork. It will have to do.

She clenches her fist around the fork and rises to a crouch. Her breath is shallow and her vision dizzies. Her laileves must be tiring, having not charged to completion during the day. She'd spent too long sleeping this afternoon.

Her jasper-enhanced ears pick up on a rustling of paper coming

The Scorched Sky

from the living room. Eiranth's legs wobble. *You did this*, she warns herself. *The one thing mother told you to do, and you couldn't even do that right.*

The cloaking spell must never be allowed to expire, Mother said, *or you'll find harthens at your door, dragging your screaming body to King Fellhearth's zeniary.* A lifetime of indentured servitude for zenites, those gifted with control of all laileve stones.

But Eiranth let them expire anyway, and now there is a harthen in her house, coming to take her to Scarafell. Strange, though, that the king would send only one harthen. Wouldn't he think to overpower her?

All she has to do is dispose of this one, and she can escape their grasp. She tightens her grip on the fork and kicks open the door, a prayer to Ausola on her lips.

Inside, it's as if a tornado has swept through the room. The opalite light hanging from the ceiling is smashed, shards of crystal scattered over the floor. Eiranth nites her carnelian, requiring its mind-body connection to traverse the spaces between the shards. Crystal in her foot is the last thing she needs. She needs this harthen *gone*, now.

The carnelian energizes her limbs, filling her with enraged strength. Ripped cushions and torn pages decorate the floor. The curtains have been pulled from their railings, and with them, great chunks of wood from the walls.

It ignites a deep, carnal rage within her. "Get the fuck out of my house!" she screams, turning towards the other side of the room.

And then she sees him.

The intruder. Dressed in a black hood and long overcoat, he's trapped between the bookshelf and Eiranth. She smirks, holding the fork out.

"You're dead," she snarls, and runs at him with the fork outstretched. The intruder cowers, stoking the rage already burning inside her. "Harthen."

She uses the carnelian's power to hurl the fork at his head. Like a frog latching onto a damselfly, the intruder's hand shoots upwards and he grabs the fork before it can penetrate his skull.

Fuck.

The Scorched Sky

Only one thing makes a person that inhumanly quick.

Carnelian.

Eiranth reels, using the vacuum of the moment to take another look at the intruder. No royal crest, no green chains, and most importantly, no gaspetite sword.

"You're not a harthen," she breathes. "If you're not--" she glowers at him. "What the fuck are you?"

There's no way she will be able to overpower him now if he is using carnelian too. They'll scramble for hours, unable to gain an upper hand. Or, she can move fast.

The intruder takes a step forward; she glances around the room and notices a paper-knife on her writing table. She lunges for it and holds it out, ready to pounce if he comes at her with the pronged fork.

This time, she cannot miss. She takes a second to steady her vision and hone in on the space above his heart. Where soon, a knife will protrude from. She narrows her eyes and pulls a slow breath into her chest, retracting her arm as she does.

But before she can do anything, all her magic dies.

Shock makes her almost drop the knife. Stars swim in her vision. Currents whirl around her and she has to close her eyes, too dizzy to see. Despite her disorientation, she knows what he's done. Because she can do it, too.

"What…" she splutters, surprise momentarily stupefying her. "Did you do that for?"

The intruder clears his throat, and she can hear the sound of metal clanging onto wood. Has he put the pronged fork on her desk? Why would he give up his weapon?

"You're more useful to me alive," the intruder says. He's got a strange accent, not the boggy wave of the Sillian Glade tone, but a sharper, craggy lilt, like the mountains that scar the country's far north.

He's from Scarafell, the capital city. Home of King Fellhearth, and all the royal zenites. Eiranth knows that accent; it read her bedtime stories, sang her songs, and taught her how to use the laileve stones in her scalp.

The Scorched Sky

So you are a harthen, she tries to say, but something stops her.

Mother told her to remain hidden. She has obeyed for twenty-three years.

Eiranth rubs her eyes and peels them open. She rests her weight on the writing table, shielding her vision with her other hand. "Get out. *Now.*"

"Please—I'm looking for this," the intruder pleads, sending his shaking hands into his jacket pocket. Who wears a long overcoat in the swamp's midsummer?

"I don't give a single sun ray," she snarls. "Get. Out." As soon as the room stops spinning, the paper-knife will slice open his neck. Anything to get him the fuck out.

"Please listen to me. Have you seen this?" From his pocket, the intruder pulls a battered lump of parchment. He unfolds the paper, revealing a drawing; it's faded from age, sun-bleached on one side, sewn together down the middle, with pencil lines and colors so weak that Eiranth can't make it out properly. The drawing is of a circle, of that she is sure, with orange swirls in its center, like fire encased in the leathery paper. As she stares at the paper, the room stops spinning. "What is it?"

"It's an orb," the intruder says plainly, as if she's supposed to be able to glean any meaning from that.

His vagueness ignites fury inside her. "There are many orbs in Silla's Glade." She pushes herself into a stand, leaning towards the drawing. "Why are you in my house?"

"Because," the intruder says, "three of these orbs exist in the world. One of them is in my bag. The other is in King Fellhearth's underground caverns. And the third one is in your house."

I am from the UK but have been living in South Korea for two years, where I rediscovered my love for writing. The Scorched Sky is my second book in as many years, currently being wrangled into something presentable.

The Scorched Sky

PHOTOFIT

By Matt Bartle

Duct tape covers the peephole in the door. The tape, matt-silver against the gloss-white, is stuck in the shape of a cross, preventing any light from permeating the darkness.

The corridor outside is rarely lit. The residents of the other apartments spend the majority of their time alone, actively avoiding their neighbours.

The walls are thin enough, and the flat is quiet enough, for the occupants to hear relays clicking whenever someone activates a light's motion sensor somewhere down the hallway.

Inside, despite the security of the electronic lock, there is a chain linking the door to the frame.

Photofit

Deep shadows form everywhere except the small bathroom where a red bulb is housed. Light blooms soft and low in the darkness. The bathroom door is only open to illuminate the flat. The rest of the apartment is lit only by screens of various sizes showing various streams of information, blinking lights at various frequencies.

He's not looking at any of it.

He sits wearing only Adidas tracksuit-bottoms and a VR headset. He presses his elbows into the chair's arms, arches his back, and peels the stuck skin from the black leather covering the chair. Wires trail up over its wheeled frame and, in places, they are stuck with the same silver tape.

The flat is stuffy from all the re-breathed air of man and machine; the windows stay shut most of the time.

Electrical cables are bunched and bound into vines, each silver-tape loop about a forearm's length from the other. The dark masses are laid out along the perimeter of the room.

Where cables cross a thoroughfare, a taut ramp of tape covers them, preventing wayward toes getting stuck and snagged in the darkness. The vines have been there long enough that they are now avoided habitually.

With his eyes closed beneath the lenses he stretches, hands in fists above his head, both his bones and the fabric creaking.

He scratches at his bare flanks.

He has the bony, hairless chest of a malnourished child; the torso of an uncooked chicken carcass.

The phone rings, and he muscle-memory answers with a grunt. Before the caller can finish their sentence, he says, "No," and hangs up.

There is a pause where the only sounds in the apartment are that of the CPU fans cooling circuitry and heating the air with the constant tinnitus of electricity.

His phone vibrates, skittering across the desk.

He grunts and sighs, removes his headset, and rubs his eyes. He picks up the phone and answers.

Photofit

There is the soft bleat of a muffled voice.

He sits forward, elbows propped on knees, eyes wide-open watching moving lights blink-blink-blinking in the darkening sky outside. "Of course," he says, "I can go now." His brow furrows, "It's close. I can be there in about fifteen minutes."

There is another short bleat.

"No," he says, "I'll be able to find her," and hangs up.

Wires are unplugged and the goggles are placed on the desk. He rests his feet beside them, his toes gripping the desk-top like a gargoyle as he looks out at the surrounding buildings. Mostly high rises like his; they crowd small communal spaces, each filled with concrete benches and low maintenance trees with patchy lawns.

His pulse beats hard behind his eyes and he realises he's been holding his breath.

He wraps his arms around his knees and lets his vision blur and his breath grow shallow.

It takes two swiping tries before he successfully grabs a

thin, plastic bottle from where he sits and, after unscrewing the cap, he taps two white pills into a palm and swallows them with a long gulp of lukewarm water from a glass that smells of chlorine and saliva.

Still perching, he reaches and flips through a pile of coloured folders before finding the correct blue one. It bends between his hands like a magician's trick deck. In the red light, it is bruise-purple.

Standing and stretching, he carries the folder to his backpack where he pushes it into an elasticated pocket behind an A4 notebook and laptop that has never been turned on.

At the doorway, he stamps on Air Max 110's and pulls on a once-white vest. He looks to the window to check for rain.

April showers, he almost says aloud and thinks, however briefly, of his grandmother saying the same thing in her own flat.

His fists clench and unclench.

He sighs, patting his pockets. He feels for his key card and leaves without his phone. The lining of his jacket is cold against the

Photofit

sweating skin of his arms.

He takes sunglasses despite the impending darkness and the late hour.

**

He hurries to meet his client not far from the apartment on a street where he can almost see the sea. There is still the occasional cry of a gull.

His tower block is still visible above the rooftops of the buildings and, as always, he stops to look back and picture his flat is on the side closest to him. Along the road there are mostly shop-fronts and takeaways; some boarded up, some with flats above the kebab shops, and some with second level storerooms full of greetings cards and deflated foil balloons.

He looks at his wrist where his watch should be and hopes he is on time. When he spots her, she is trying, with moderate success, to eat noodles without her elbows being knocked by passers-by. She sits on an upturned beer crate as a makeshift stool. Her dark glasses reflect the brightly lit, striped canopy above. With each chewed mouthful, red and white stripes move across the lenses like a barber's pole.

Although they haven't met, he knows her from photographs.

He knows of her by reputation.

Others may know her by the reputation of her mother.

Rain has started to fall but the streets are still hot and busy. The extra humidity intensifies the smells; wet jackets and miso and rubber and beer; old umbrellas damp like bad breath; the constant oil slick of frying food both savoury and sweet.

"Miss Hardy?" he says.

The scars on her face are half-hidden by glasses and the angular cut of her straight, dark, hair.

"So formal," she says, "Mae is fine."

Nodding, he says he has been sent to speak with her.

He starts to talk and, giving up, raises his voice above the

Photofit

sound of the rain now drumming against the awning. He says, "Would you like to go somewhere quieter? Somewhere with less people?"

Her head tilts to one side as she stops chewing.

She stabs the chopsticks into something meaty, swallows, and says, "Sure."

The rain falls in waves, alternating between light and heavy.

She says, "Where to? You live nearby? Maybe we could go to your place, and you can talk me through what you've found?"

They watch themselves in each other's glasses. Behind her glasses her gaze is unwavering. He sees the reflected dissonance of his own face as he searches for an excuse. He opens and closes his mouth, eventually nodding for her to follow.

She stands, brushing her hands over the ripped black denim covering her thighs, and says, "Lead the way, handsome."

His cheeks flush.

She leaves the uneaten noodles still steaming on the crate.

She says, "I was expecting somebody older."

They set off slowly in the drizzle, increasing their pace as the rain intensifies.

She says, "You look about twelve."

He looks away, squinting into the dying light.

"I wasn't expecting someone ancient," she says, "But someone a little more grizzled. Maybe someone wearing something other than a backpack and trackies."

With his eyes anywhere but on her, he says, "I'm just a Runner." Seeing her blank expression, he says, "I just give out the information."

They move in near silence until they arrive at his flat.

The rain keeps falling as the sun sets but her dark glasses stay on.

Photofit

***

After removing his jacket, he kicks off his shoes and sets them on the mat by the door. She doesn't. If questioned, she could blame the laces running up to her knees, but she wouldn't.

He takes the folder from his bag and motions for her to follow him into the apartment. She steps forward and closes the door behind her.

She removes her sunglasses and hangs them from the opening of her t-shirt. Her hands slide into her jacket pockets. She says, "Not much of a talker, are you?"

She stands with her back to the doorway and watches him walk away from her. In the quiet, she can hear his bare feet sticking and peeling from the polished concrete as he walks.

She says, "Have you actually got any lights?" Her breath bounces back from her upturned collar as she scans the room. She twists her neck from side to side until she feels it pop.

He stands beside a small table and places the folder on it.

She says, "Are you sure you've got enough cables?"

He sighs, "The wires are a necessity; my setup still isn't right, but the rent's cheap. I figured the landlord doesn't want me kicking holes in the walls and rewiring. What you're looking at is, at best, a temporary solution."

Mae's eyes follow the gnarled, black roots running around the perimeter of the room to a bank of blinking lights behind a perforated steel screen. There are odd branches climbing up the walls where wires spread like ivy leading to nothing.

Despite the apparent chaos the room is scented by the calming ozone-smell of hot electronics and of rice steam and fabric detergent.

In what little light there is, Mae's eyes roam and linger on the kitchen area.

She sees his teapot. It is set out on the worktop beside a solo ceramic cup.

In that single object she pictures his entire life. A life of silence and tea leaves and copper-bottomed pans; spatulas burned

Photofit

from gas flames; books made of paper stacked in irregular piles on benches and on tables; a futon only large enough for one.

"Would you like a drink?" he says, and the sudden noise makes the image slip and Mae's fists clench.

She shakes her head.

He runs a hand over his close-cropped hair, flicking rainwater from his fingers and onto the floor.

Against the glow of the red light, he stands like a shadow.

She stands against the white of the doorway like a void.

He pinches water from the tip of an ear and says, "Would you like to sit down?" He looks at the coffee table, "I don't usually meet people in person," he says, "Let alone entertain."

Mae sets out towards the futon, more out of curiosity than fatigue. She stops and stands in the centre of the room, "What's with the red light?"

She cranes her neck but stays put.

She can see the lines strung between the walls and little hooks drilled into grouting. Over the sink and over the bath there are temporary shelves made of what looks like plywood.

"It's for my bathroom-slash-darkroom."

"A darkroom?" she says, "You develop pictures? Real pictures with actual paper?" Her teeth are bright despite the darkness.

He chews his bottom lip, clears his throat, and picks up the folder and says, "Would you like to read the file?"

She says, "No."

She says, "Skip to the end."

He puts the folder down and pushes it away with splayed fingers. His shoulders drop as he shakes his head, "He's not who you're looking for."

He steps out of the red again, backing further into the low-glow of the screens and the shadows. He sits on his chair, folds his legs beneath him, and watches. With a bent finger, he scrapes

Photofit

gathering water from under his chin.

He says, "He didn't even know your Ma before you were born. I'm sorry, but he's not your Da."

They wait three silent breaths before Mae raises her eyebrows and says, "That's it?"

He looks at the table. At the folder. At its brevity.

"Pretty much," he says. "I don't know anything more. I can't tell you who your actual father is, only about the fella you told us to investigate."

Her face hangs slack, her eyes blink-blink-blinking.

He says, "You did say: skip to the end."

She says, "I paid you to find him. I paid you a lot." She sighs, closing her eyes, "How can buying information be so expensive, and so little fun? How come there's nothing to show for my money?"

He says, "Some people don't want to be found."

All her pent-up nerves, all her energy, is distilled into tensing muscles and grinding teeth. Her nose-skin bunches and the faintest twitch passes through her top lip. She opens her eyes, breathing out long and smooth and slow.

She speaks quietly, her voice soft and measured, "What have I paid you people for?" With her jaw clenched, and her eyes to the ground, she says, "For you to tell me one person isn't the one I'm looking for? Out of how many? Where're the actual results? Where are the actual details?"

Her body seems to have changed, she looks different, like someone he can't quite place.

Across the room he looks small and hunched, his fingers clasped around his ankles, already out of his depth and already out of excuses.

Holding up his hands, his voice small, he says, "I just provide the paperwork."

"Paperwork?" Her voice is barely there, just the sound of teeth parting in the air. She says, "That folder looks pretty thin to me. It doesn't look like you provide very much paper."

Photofit

Her eyes are bright as they meet his gaze.

There is a squeak of wet rubber as she steps forward and he catches himself flinching.

And then he realises; she's transformed. She's just like her mother.

"Tell me," she says, her voice quiet and calm, and her face set hard, "You might not know who my father is, but do you know my mother?"

She keeps walking towards him.

He nods and he can feel the weight of the knowledge shift from his head to his sinking heart and he knows she sees it too.

"The apple didn't fall very far from the tree, Jakob."

His brow creases, "Who told…" He can barely shake his head. He feels his heartbeat thudding in his ears and says, "I'm nobody. I'm just a layer. I'm security."

"Security?" she says, "It doesn't look like you can handle yourself."

Bardsy 2023 Fall Anthology — First Chapters

"Not like that," he says, "I'm no bouncer. I'm expendable."

"You're paid to be a pawn?"

He says, "Not well."

Mae says, "I'm disappointed. I actually thought you were going to do a better job."

He opens his mouth for a second before she swings a ringed fist of knuckles that connects flat against his temple. Jakob drops from the chair with the crack of an eye socket on polished concrete.

She is behind him as he tries to rise.

His legs tangle.

Mae's forearm is already pressing against his windpipe.

He kicks out against the chair, swinging himself onto his back and pressing his weight onto her as she wriggles beneath him. She holds tight, riding out the thrashing. Rug-burned blood streaks under his busted heel as he flails, hissing like a cornered cat.

Photofit

He stops.

Goes limp.

His breathing is shallow just beyond her ear.

They embrace in the silence, and she lets out a sigh as they lie in the red glow and the smell of scorched metal.

In the silence of the flat, the rain against the windows is hurricane-loud.

Mae waits a breath before rolling him off her chest and onto his belly.

Jakob's entire weight rocks on his chest as she wraps his wrists and his ankles with lengths of duct tape torn from a roll she finds nearby; layers upon layers of matt-silver, dark against white skin, forming tight little croissant cuffs.

She pulls some wires from the chair and ties them around his throat like a leash, or a noose, and lays the excess in a reel where she can reach it.

Sitting cross-legged on the rug she listens to the blood bubbling over his nostril. In the redness of the light, the trail is almost invisible.

Mae checks over his eyebrow, gently rubbing the cut with a thumb. She stops and sniffs at its slickness. It is the same colour as her nail varnish. She puts her thumb into her mouth and sucks it until her thumbprint crinkles and the metallic taste has gone.

It is some time before Jakob's awake enough to be able to look up at her. His eye darkened with a purple-swelling hematoma, already so big with blood.

The sound of the rain has dimmed to an ignorable white-noise.

He lets out a small, pained grunt.

Shuffling in close, head bent down to almost meet his, she says, "I've had some time to think." She straightens, looking out of the window from an angle where she can only see the sky. "I know I have a temper. I was upset. I apologise."

If there was no rain, she might be able to see stars.

Photofit

No other flats are illuminated.

"In hindsight," she says, "This may have been a bad way of asking for your assistance, but now we've started down a path.

"You see, Jakob, I need to find him. I need to find him fast. I'm going to take what I'm owed from that deadbeat.

"Your employers need to know I'm unhappy. They need to know that I want what I'm owed."

She sits watching his still form lying the length of the futon.

He speaks quietly into the carpet, "I don't get in touch with them, they contact me."

She huffs out long and slow from her nose, and says, "Then we'll just have to wait till they get worried."

With his jaw pressed to the floor he blinks to clear his vision. He tests the limits of his shoulder's movements followed by pinched arm-hairs and the crackle of glue.

He flinches when his phone buzzes across the desk. The wire against his throat pulls infinitesimally tighter.

Once sculptor, now mechanic. Aspiring writer and maker.

Photofit

THE TIME BETWEEN US

By L.A. Redding

EMILY

(I think, maybe) A Day Not Too Long Ago

I don't know what tipped me off that this week would be different, less learned and more improv, but it's why I chose to wait for my ride here and not at home, which according to Google Maps is one-quarter mile in my rearview. Here, where the street is one straight line in either direction—no side roads, no intersections, no alleys. Here, where the more mature street is perfumed with the sweetness of cherry blossoms in full bloom and lined with century-old oaks and Victorians, restored to their original luster, the sun-dappled neighborhood that borders mine not yet overrun with camera crews.

The Time Between Us

Last night I changed the usual "meet-me-at-the-end-of-the-block" location, to the next street over, shadowed by the tallest backyard fence in a three-block radius. I feel safer here, less exposed, sheltered from curious eyes and inevitable scrutiny that would trigger when seeing our front door hanging off its hinges, the manicured lawn overrun with tire marks and flooded with water from the sprinkler system. And my favorite teddy bear lying face down in the muck, one arm twisted awkwardly behind its back. Blaring sirens converged, early this morning, before the sun rose over Pleasant Valley on the outskirts of Syracuse, the New York Baker Street address surely readying itself for headline news. It's the only memory I can dig up. The only memory that doesn't trigger in me a thousand questions and no ready answers. A darkness from which I might not recover.

No one in the world knows how this feels. Not even me.

EDIN

The Horrible Feeling of Now

Breathing. I can't remember spending any time thinking about that. Why would I? I mean, every damn day it's this one thing you can't do without. The one thing that makes everything else possible.

The square room is drained of animation, its walls whitewashed, and mirror-like floor still wet around the perimeter from the janitor's mop. My nose tingles with whatever disinfecting cocktail sleeves every surface, the bitter metallic taste coating my tongue. I swallow, allowing the sensation to burn my throat, ignoring the glass of water sitting on the bedside table, but unable to forget the gaping chasm that has opened in my life. Now, breathing is the only thing that matters, the only thing that exists between me and that moment when I realized I made the wrong choice. All of this would be different. And breathing would still be this thing that happens, in the background, all-important and completely unnoticed. Instead, the world goes on in all the ways that no longer matter to me.

My eyes find the precise slit between the oaks where the sun usually rises, the one I've witnessed for two long weeks. That momentary and undefinable space when everything seems to be on pause, like the world is in between breaths—and my feeling of kinship with it. But I won't see it today. The sun.

Outside the window, trees are beginning to sway with the coming gale. Following each gust, autumn leaves disembark and surrender

The Time Between Us

to the ground. For now, it's just the intermittent *plink-plunk* of rain on the glass.

But the gathering storm is not what I hear. It's the steady, methodical beep of a machine. Like every machine, it serves a purpose, starting from pieces and parts—gears and switches, bolts and bits and springs and loose wire. But it also has a sort of brain. A computer. The thing that holds it all together depends on the breath that is electricity, impulse, and code-seeking. A signal is sent. The machine does the job it's programmed to do.

During the long hours of my self-imposed late-night shift, Wikipedia and Google have become raison d'etre, offering their easy companionship, all the twists and turns serving as balm for my wound. And for my hopefulness. This hour's search term: "machines." The one in this room, displaying numbers for flow, pressure, and volume, was conceived of by a nineteenth- century French engineer and physician, who answered the need of balloonists and mountain climbers when they ascended beyond the levels where oxygen was sufficient for breathing. One steel-spiked boot after another I imagine echoing off the mountainside, and my unwavering concentration, the weight of sore muscles, perspiration wetting my face and neck, anticipating the apex. And a balloon cruising above the clouds with each hot breath, my

Pajama-Clad-Bad- Hair-Day Lego Self floating away to some distant landmark. It's weird. The way a machine has become this connection I can't break. The invention I might embrace, or possibly punch and kick back into its innocent parts, if only my body would unglue from this utilitarian chair, which according to one of my minimized windows is categorized as "modern guest seating."

The lights flicker. I set aside my laptop, holding steady at twenty-one percent battery power. But I think I know.

Soon the coast will be battered with inflated seas, the invisible breath slamming, receding, slamming again, removing chinks from its armor.

***

EMILY

My dad's applying to work at Finish Line, and not the neighboring town's fancy tri-level mall location, but the one local's christened "the dead mall," because a man overdosed in the parking lot. Dad wants us to call our new city The Hub of the Universe. *It's classier*, he tells me and my two sisters while driving us to the mall through

The Time Between Us

the outskirts of Boston, glancing over to check our reactions. Half of me is still in bed. I didn't sleep much last night. But even I can recognize the morbid irony of it all.

The Great Ironic Joke has us sharing Dad's newly downsized pickup truck, which doesn't allow room to spread out, so we're squished together on one bench seat. He returned the luxury, all leather Chevy Suburban on loan from the DOD, the employer he quit without so much as a family memo. The SUV provided ample space with three rows of seats, giving us at least the appearance of privacy. Now, every time Dad shifts gears, his elbow knocks into my knee. Beside me, Kaitlin's staring at the ceiling. It's what she does when preparing a speech. Renée's reading her new Advanced Calculus syllabus, which is, so far, eleven pages long. I've been counting each page she turns. Counting helps me to focus on something other than what my mind keeps bringing up against my will.

In the fifteen minutes we've been on the road, the radio hasn't been able to pick up any stations. Dad stops hitting scan and turns off the power button, but it must not be working. Static continues, fading in and out.

"Anyway," Dad says. "I have a theory about the Hub of the Universe.

Would you like to hear it, ladies?"

We're giving him the silent treatment. Not like it'll work, but at least it's something.

This morning Dad shaved for the first time since he quit his job. It's nice being able to see the lower half of his face again. I was beginning to think he'd turn into a beard carrying around a body. His black hair is speckled with gray that seems to have sprouted overnight. He removes his baseball cap, places it in his lap and rubs his knuckles across his forehead so hard I think a layer of skin might peel away.

The Red Sox cap is new, a Goodwill price tag still stuck to the brim. He set aside his pride at being a lifelong Yankees fan, said he was *taking one for the team*. My sisters and I agreed not to tell him about the tag. We're not exactly on team Boston, which has nothing to do with baseball.

Kaitlin reaches for her headphones, the ones she bought with her own money. Renée yawns. I glance through September's issue of Collegiate Track and Field magazine, the one I rescued from our mailbox before we left Syracuse, chewing on my last fingernail, the middle one on my left hand, the rest already ragged. Hopefully, it'll

The Time Between Us

keep me from using that finger in another, much more inappropriate way. I'm tired. Edgy. I just might tell Dad how I really feel. For me, it'd be a miracle, but, hey, it could happen.

"Oh, come on, girls," Dad says. "Don't worry. This retail gig is a temporary solution. Just until I can build a customer base for my painting jobs."

Dad could have completed an online application, so this drive to the mall is a part of whatever hidden agenda he's forcing on us. Sure, he's smart and clever and has a Yale PhD. But a twenty-year career wearing a suit for his government job didn't exactly prepare him to start a business, so this is way weird, surreal even.

Dad says, louder this time, "Alright, my progeny, the sweet and sour sum of my loins."

"Watch out for the crass attack," Renée says.

"Really?" Kaitlin stops adjusting her headphones. "Seriously lame, Dad."

"Don't be gross." I whack his arm with my magazine.

"Good," he says. "Now that I have your attention. Imagine a downtown billboard in neon lights. Your favorite pop culture hero. Go, Emily."

His question feels like a gut punch. I was supposed to be trying out for Syracuse High's track team tomorrow, something I've been planning since seventh grade, but it suffered what Renée would call a strike-through, one of many lately. But I can't change my answer.

Staring at the floor, I say, "Duh. Flo-Jo." Or Jackie Joyner-Kersee. Jim Thorpe would work, too, the first Indigenous American athlete to win Olympic track and field gold medals. Sure. There's this shared athletic connection despite the decades that separate us and our different surnames, but I also feel a cultural and ethnic relationship that can't be undone, no matter my mixed heritage.

Renée says, "Diane Sawyer."

Kaitlin lifts her headphones enough for us to hear the opening chorus of Harry Styles' newly released cover of "Sign of the Times." She sings alongside his falsetto, spreading out her arms like she's flying.

Dad says, "Did you know our new city consists of layers, the parts

The Time Between Us

you can see and the parts you can't?"

He insists Boston is more than concrete and steel and glass and pothole-ridden streets. More than the dizzying heights of skyscrapers, which boggle the eyes and brain into thinking they, and the circumstances that built them, are infinite. Not like anyone is asking me, but I think it's only because of all the morning haze, advancing from the Charles River and settling upon everything. The Hub of the Universe theory doesn't provide any answers to our immediate situation, but that's how our dad thinks, how he handles the situation, not better, just different.

Kaitlin removes her headphones, cradles them in her lap. "Too bad I can't check the weather." She emphasizes each word in a ho-hum rhythm, twisting her long auburn hair into a knot on top of her head. There's no sign of her Cosmo mag, and she's not wearing makeup today, which is basically her SOS flag.

She continues, "Or check the time. Or... really, anything at all." She releases her hair like a visual exclamation point.

I know she misses Michael, her boyfriend who lives in the city we left behind. More like fled. It must be hard not being able to talk to him. Or text. I get it even though I don't have a boyfriend. Or any friends. Not anymore. So far, freshman year sucks the big sucking suckage.

Renée says, "Three hundred and fifty-six point-four miles. Doesn't quite seem far enough, does it?"

Her sarcasm is new but just as sharp as everything else about her. Renée's specialty is climbing every ladder presented, so I'm guessing this must be extra humiliating for her. But I know better than to respond, because it's not Kaitlin she's thinking about. Or even our recent exit from upper middle-class life in New York. I know she's thinking about yesterday. And last week. And the months leading up to yesterday that prefaced everything, even the seat cushion spring poking into my backside right now. The one I'm about to rip out of the seat and chuck out the window.

I'd rather forget the comedy of horrors—a blur of fleeting images, the horrible feeling of being homeless, my missing clothes and books and magazines, the best of which was my two-year collection of Collegiate Track and Field magazine. I don't know why I'm expecting the clown to come out of the closet. Maybe it's the hope I have of seeing my mother again. The bit of her that remains intact, her sweetness and charm and innocent Dorothy-on-the-yellow-brick- road doppelgänger prettiness.

The Time Between Us

My sisters are nesting dolls of our mother, except for their dark blue eyes, while I'm the oddball who resembles Dad with his Iroquois roots. Like we represent the dividing line between Kansas and Oz. And that's just outer appearances.

But tech downsizing is something we now have in common. Weirdly, it makes me feel closer to my sisters, like we're finally from the same family, fighting the same fight, seeking the same justice. Sure, to an outsider it might seem small scale, but my sisters and I are lost without our smartphones, our family plan fully in the rearview as of last week. That's what happens when your father confiscates your devices, without warning or explanation. I've been grounded plenty of times, but this is not like that. This feels more like a part of me is missing. So, yeah, we're kinda pissed, silently fuming and regrouping while we search for another way around Dad's personal firewall.

Kaitlin's woe-is-me attitude and Renée's sarcastic take on our situation might be prying a crack in Dad's façade. Pit sweat is not his best look, but who can blame him for being nervous? He's applying for a job that pays eight bucks an hour. Or maybe it's just the late August mid-morning heat, which has snuck up on us and we can't use the truck's air conditioning because a sour fish smell emanates from the vents every time we turn on the fan. The previous owner must've been a fisherman. Or a mutinous octopus. I send a silent apology to Squidward.

Despite the promising shift in Dad's approach, his good morning soliloquy isn't working. Kaitlin turns up the volume on her headphones, and Renée buries her face in her AP calculus textbook. I know it's weird, but I think about the last YouTube video I watched, a documentary on whales.

Without looking up from her textbook, Renée says, "Your description of the city reminds me of newspaper production. The paper shows up every day, and you can hold it in your hands, or, if you're like most people, read it *online*..." She pauses and stares at Dad's profile. "Yet readers are typically oblivious to what goes on behind the scenes."

For a second, I think Dad might give in, tell us we can have our phones back. He glances at Renée with his *holy shit!* face twerk, but nothing she says shocks any of us. If she were to be written into a *Transformer* movie, as an intellectual archetype in Dad's Hub of the City theorem, she'd be "Teen Journalist to Penthouse Suite."

Dad says, "Nice observation, Renny Penny." He stretches his palm out and she taps it while turning a textbook page with her other

The Time Between Us

hand. They're always in sync, like two people sharing one brain. His mood is light. But for me it's a hard sell.

"You guys are scary," I say, wondering about the dark night that swallowed our mother, like a mouth that is a whale gaping and gathering everything in its path; plankton and schools of fish and maybe an occasional athletic field of kelp and seaweed soup, swept along with sphincter muscles, pulsing and relaxing. It isn't like Dad doesn't know our mother is missing from our family equation, so why do I feel the need to remind him?

Before I can stop the words or at least censor their content, I hear myself ask, "Where's Mom? When will she be coming home?"

My voice sounds strange, like my younger self bobbed to the surface, all naïve and stupid, unaware of the whale in the room. Or in this case, the Fish Mobile. Renée swivels her head. Is she staring at me? Or Dad? Heat flushes my face. I can't look at her, because I know what will be lurking behind her intense blue eyes and knitted brow and lips drawn down on either side. I've seen it too many times lately. A face that says she sees me as some broken thing in need of fixing.

Laura is an emerging writer of fiction, including a short story collection, "Dinos R Us," and two YA novels, "Newt Generation" and "Starting Block," which was a quarterfinalist in the 2020 Booklife Prize for Fiction contest. Her short story, "A & P and the Forever Sky," earned an honorable mention from the 2016 Writer's Digest Short-Short Story Competition. Laura enjoys nomadic life and is currently exploring the Oregon coast with Frisbee, her 21-year-old cat. Alias: Random Joy Facilitator.

The Time Between Us

THE TALISH TRILOGY: CHANGES

By Jocelyn Coleman

I fire a blast of magic from my palm. The electrical buzz flows from inside my body and to my fingertips like the low strum of a guitar. I concentrate it into a ball in the center of my palm and aim the dark blue blast towards a tree trunk. The magic leaves a black singed circle in the wood and a smile brushes my cheeks.

I've been coming to this small forest behind my home for years to practice. I stare at the training target that I've carved and hung from a different tree. The small piece of bark flaps in the breeze. I concentrate, trying to imagine there is nothing surrounding my target. My hand shoots up and my magic comes out in a thick beam of light. The wood spins with the impact, celebrating my minor victory with its little dance. Adrenaline and pride rush through me.

The Talish Trilogy: Changes

Focus, Natsu, I say to myself. *You didn't come here to practice this.*

My rolling targets are next and I roll up my sleeves. I back up and take a run at one target that I've tied to the side of a tree. I keep my eyes on it until the last possible moment before tumbling into a roll. When I'm coming out of it, my eyes draw to my target, but my short dark hair gets into my face and I miss.

Cursing, I stand back up, brushing the crisp autumn leaves off of my clothes. I try a few more times, but each time, my eyes can't lock onto the target long enough and my magic fires off-kilter. I groan and wheeze, my body getting physically and magically drained. Like a sore muscle, I need time to heal up with food and rest.

A small scar on my left forearm just below my elbow crease catches my attention then before I lower my sleeves. I run my thin fingers up it, remembering the searing pain like it was yesterday. Another non-magical student took a pair of scissors during craft time in kindergarten to my arm, wanting to see if our blood was a different colour. I learned long ago that they want us to be seen as different, as monsters because of something we were born with. No matter how hard the government tries to hide it and pretend there is peace among our streets, it is still us against them. It will always be us against them until something changes. From that day, I vowed never to be seen as weak or insignificant; so I train and hone my skills to be ready for anything they can throw at me.

Just then, my watch alarm beeps. I shake the ignorant and discriminatory thoughts from my head. I was raised better than that and I hate thinking that way, but sometimes the inevitable thoughts creep their way in.

I grab my backpack, make my way out of the woods and head to school. It wouldn't look good on my high school record to be late in my senior year again and I already have a pretty lousy track record. I take out a bagel from my backpack and munch on it as I walk. The skies are grey today and I feel a few raindrops as I exit from the shielded layer of trees. It's that awkward time between the summer and fall; school has recently started again and the rain has welcomed its way into our city. Though the murky days can get long and dreary, I still love living in North Talish.

The chubby, vibrant trees and shrubbery guide my route, sending a sense of safety and protection through me. I glance up at the massive height of some of the trees, wondering how long they have been standing. It's extraordinary to think about something living that long. With our magic, it's not like we can do such things as cast a spell to make us live forever or to raise the dead. It just doesn't

The Talish Trilogy: Changes

work that way in our bodies. Some believe it's a form of God or a higher-up being, some believe it's just science and that's how our magical genes are made up. There are just some things that Crafters can't do. Everyone has to have limitations.

By the time I get to school, it's pouring. The cool rain smells like the blossomed flowers that perish with the change of seasons. My short ebony hair sticks to my cheeks and I hope that what little makeup I wear hasn't smeared across my face. The halls are almost empty and I know that I'm going to be late. Lo and behold, a bell rings. I run to my first class, my shoes letting out a horrendous squeak as my feet shuffle on the linoleum.

"Late again, Ms. Kerning?" Mrs. Myers says as I barrel in.

I must look like a wreck. I'm drenched and panting, the heat emitting from my face. The various snickers from my classmates echo in my ears and I make my way to my desk beside the window.

My best friend, Karina, leans into me, her long blonde hair waving over her shoulder. "Were you in the woods again?"

I glance down and notice the mud stains on my jeans. I nod at her as I scramble to get my books out of my bag and remove my wet sweater.

"Why do you do that so often?" she asks me. "It's not like you're going to be fighting anyone anytime soon."

It has been over seven hundred years that Mortals (or Mors) and wizards (or Crafters) have lived in harmony. After the Great Magical War, everyone in Talish agreed to peace. Or so the government would like us to believe.

Though there isn't any inkling of another war coming, I can't help but feel it in my gut that something is coming. And isn't it better to be safe than sorry? I feel much safer knowing that I can protect my loved ones if anything ever did happen. I've never been the type to sit on the sidelines, not if I can help somebody. It's why my mother keeps trying to convince me to become a nurse or doctor, but my healing magic is lousy. She has been nagging about it more lately because I've just started my senior year and my inevitable decision to figure out a career is beginning to loom over me.

Mrs. Myers speaks, but I'm not listening. My mind wanders to other ideas.

What will I do after this year? Do I go to college or take a break?

The Talish Trilogy: Changes

The drops of rain fall lightly against the windowpane as I consider the future. Outside, the rain sprinkles on the open grass field and leaves small droplets on the cars in the parking lot. A boy breaks me out of my trance and catches my attention as he drives into one of the empty stalls and gets out, his black hair glistening with the newly laid drops of rain. Even from here, I can feel his magical energy and my heart quickens. He is about to turn around when I hear Mrs. Myers' booming voice call to me.

"Natsu?"

I jump at her call and turn to look at her.

"Are you paying attention to our history lesson? We have a test next week."

The muffled giggles of the other students dig into my ears as I nod.

"Would you mind reciting the Laws of Magic so I know you were listening?"

I quickly look back out the window, but the boy is long gone. A soft sigh escapes my lips and I return my rattled brain to class.

"Magic can neither heal nor revive the terminally ill or dying, for death needs to occur in order for there to be new life," I recite robotically, the Laws being forced into my head since I was a child.

As I speak, I hear a slight groan from a fellow student behind me, but I continue.

"Magic cannot be used to create nor manipulate love or affection. It cannot control the passage of time. Magic has many different forms such as Offensive, Defensive, and Ordinary Magic. If one abuses magic to harm Mors or others or partakes in the Dark Arts, that person, or persons will be greatly punished."

I stumble before continuing and look down at my history book, and the words leaping up at me: "greatly punished". The words repeat in my head like a perpetually swelling drumbeat. My breath becomes more rapid as my magic flows uncontrollably through me. Sweat moistens my palms as I hear those words again and again, the drum penetrating my skull. I close my eyes to try and stop the dizziness, but I can't stand it anymore.

My hands slam on my desk and a wave of air ripples throughout the classroom. The other student's hair and clothes flow with the huge gust of wind I've created and loose papers scatter all around.

The Talish Trilogy: Changes

There are random gasps that fill the silence as they take in what it is I've just done.

"Natsu!" I hear Mrs. Myers scream. My eyes open to all the scared faces. Magic is forbidden in the classroom.

"I-I'm sorry," I stagger out. "I'm fine, I swear." Mrs. Myers looks startled, but stern. I compose myself, taking several deep breaths, and she moves on to continue her lesson.

"Now, as we all know, the Laws of Magic were established after the war," she goes on to explain. "And certain economical changes happened once peace was declared. Can anyone tell me what some of those changes were?"

One of my classmates raises their hand. "Each sector was divided and is responsible for some sort of value they can contribute to society."

"Such as?" Mrs. Myers asks.

"Our sector of Talish is renowned for its agriculture. We are the farming capital of the sectors. North Talish supplies most of the fresh food to the rest of the world."

But in turn, that limits the careers the people here can pursue, I think to myself. The majority of people tend to become farmers, unless they work in the city. I'm uncertain yet of what I want to do, but I know it's not farming.

Mrs. Myers proceeds drearily with her history lesson, and again my eyes are drawn to the window, hoping to see something exciting or that the boy has returned to his car. But there is nothing. I catch a glimpse of my reflection instead.

My small pale arms reflect in the glass underneath the mud. My black hair lightly caresses the tops of my shoulders. I have never been much into fashion or updating my looks. I keep my hair short so that I don't have to do any maintenance on it except brush it into a straight and presentable look. I use minimal makeup, mostly around my eyes. I have always been very proud of my eyes- a bright emerald green that seem to shine. They are the only gift from my father that I kept.

The bell rings which breaks me from my trance and notice students pile out of the classroom. I slowly pack up my books when I feel a hand on my shoulder. When I spin around, Karina is hovering over me. Her long golden hair flows down her back and waves side to side as she speaks.

The Talish Trilogy: Changes

Before she can start though, one of her other gorgeous friends comes up to us.

"Karina, are we going to the mall today?" she asks.

Karina wraps her arms around my shoulders. "Can't. I have to hang out with my best friend."

"I thought I was your best friend?" she teases.

"Fine. My oldest friend then."

"Hey," I chirp. "I'm younger than you."

"What do you people want from me?" she groans. We chuckle and her friend says she'll see Karina later. Seeing her with her other friends always makes me feel so out of place. I don't match any of those beautiful people obsessed with makeup and boys. On paper, Karina and I are polar opposites. If we hadn't met when we were kids, I wonder if we would still be friends today?

"Cupcake?" she says to me once she says her good-byes to her friend, handing me a small container. "You look like you need one today."

I take it and open the lid. There is a small fluffy cupcake with light blue icing on top. Placed on the icing is a little sugar flower that I'm assuming she made by hand. "Your baking skills always seem to astound me. Thank you." I take a bite. Delicious, of course.

She shifts her curvy hips, her loose flower skirt waving with them, and her large red lips break into a smile. "Are we hanging out today?" she asks me, her bright blue eyes staring into mine.

"I can't, I have Magical Arts training remember?"

A look of disappointment covers her face. "Natsu, come on! You're at school all day and then you spend another two hours after, learning what?"

"Offensive and Defensive magic—" I begin.

"Exactly! Useless stuff!"

She doesn't get it because she's a Mortal. My thoughts race to her lack of power before I can halt them.

She leans lightly on the desk behind her, her chest being pressed up as she does so. I glance behind her and notice one of the boys

The Talish Trilogy: Changes

staring at her for a moment before he exits the room. I roll my eyes.

"You're seventeen; you need to be out and about in the world! To explore places! We can even go beyond the gate into West Talish! It's so easy to get to the border from here."

She's always loved adventure and meeting new people. Her new mission the last few weeks has been to travel across the border into West Talish. I don't know what she expects to find over there, but almost every day she talks about going.

"It's Friday, we need adventure!" She grabs my bag as a hostage.

"Karina…"

"Please, oh please?" She's begging now? Something's up with her.

"What's over there?" I know she wouldn't press this hard for a simple adventure.

She pauses and bites her lip. "There's this guy…"

I knew it! I contemplate my options. If I go, my mom may kill me. If I stay, Karina may stop speaking to me. Neither option is a good one.

My tired body makes the decision for me though.

I smile at her. "You're going to have to explain my training absence to Canisha."

"You're not more worried about your mom?"

"Oh, I am, but at least you can take the blame for one of them."

She chuckles then, knowing my Magical Arts instructor is the lesser of the two evils. "Deal."

"And if my mom murders me, I am coming back to haunt you for the rest of your days."

Though Karina is ecstatic, I can't help but have a bad feeling in the pit of my stomach about this trip.

* * *

Luckily the rain has stopped and we walk over to the border that is about twenty minutes away from our school. Once there, we make our way to the line where we show our identification on the inside of our wrists. It indicates which area of Talish we are from and if we have magic or don't. I look down at the black ink embedded into my skin that reads "NORTH, CRAFTER".

Since the War, there have been mixed children of Crafters and Mors; much to some conservative people's disgust. Their tattoos would say "NORTH, MIX, NM" for "non-magical" or "M" for "magical". It's really a gamble with genetics to whether the child will be magical or not, but if they are, everyone has to know it.

I stand in the line next to Karina, between the black ropes and poles that indicate where to go. We move forward slowly, waiting for everyone else to be scanned and searched for anything suspicious. There's a long line of guards as we approach, sitting at little desks to put your bags onto. A metal archway sits beside each station that we cross through to scan for any weapons before the guard searches us on the other side.

We get to the front of the line and I go first. I look at the border guard as I walk through the giant scanner. He investigates my backpack to find my school books and supplies. They usually check for anything that could be used to make spells: herbs, pieces of wood, chalk; anything dangerous among Crafters.

The guards give Karina and me the all clear and let us cross through to the other side of the building, exiting into West Talish. Karina leads me to a train right beside the border and we get in. For the whole forty-five minutes, Karina looks like she's about to jump out of her skin. She rambles on about this guy and how they met when she came up here with her dad on one of his work trips. I drift in and out of what she's saying, noticing a Crafter using magic to run the train in the next car.

"Hey," Karina hums beside me. "That's not going to be you, you know."

She knows me too well. "But that's mostly how it goes these days- Crafters being put to 'good use' with their magic in jobs that benefit the Nation. We're builders, farmers, engineers, mechanics, really anything with labour that the Mors don't want to do. We don't get to do the fun jobs, Karina."

"You sound like Mrs. Myers," she complains. "Just because you can do it, doesn't mean you have to. Did you think more about what your mom said about being a doctor?"

I scoff and play with the cuffs of my sleeve. "That's not for me," I tell her. "I don't want to watch people die."

The Talish Trilogy: Changes

"But you'd also be helping people."

I cross my arms over my torso. "I don't know. I'd rather work more on my Offensive magic than my healing magic."

"But why? There's no career in that unless you want to be a Magical Arts trainer like your mom."

My face scrunches up at the idea. "I don't know if I want to do that either."

She rests her hand gently on my leg. "That's okay. You don't need to know what you want to do right now. But I know either way, you'll do something great."

I give her a tired smile. "Thanks, Karina."

She doesn't get it though. As a Crafter, our lives are basically already planned out for us. With few career paths, there's only so far a Crafter can go for their future. Since the Great War, Crafters are a few to a dozen compared to Mors, leaving them to make most of the decisions for us, and we have just gotten into the systematic rhythm of following along with the crowd.

The train stops and Karina lets out a little squeal. She's looking through the window at someone. As the doors open, she jumps into the arms of some guy. He's tall with dark features and wraps his arms around her like a baby holding onto a teddy bear. They kiss, and I turn away in embarrassment. Oh great, now for an evening of being the awkward third wheel.

As if sensing my thoughts, Karina breaks from him and turns to me. "Natsu, this is Kenjamin. Don't worry though, he's brought a friend."

Kenjamin moves out of the way to reveal another boy standing behind him. He has dark brown hair with tinges of blonde hidden in it that lighten his features and his shadowy eyes. His hair falls loosely around his forehead, grazing his skin. He is about the same height as Kenjamin, and has a strong build, like he could be a hunter in another life. The way he stares at me makes me uncomfortable, like he's trying to analyze me from the inside. I look away timidly, trying to hide at least some of my secrets.

Karina quickly comes in. "This is Taye."

Taye from Talish? I think to myself and almost break out into a chuckle, but quickly cover it with a cough.

The Talish Trilogy: Changes

I glance back his way then and he's smiling too. In an instant, I'm at ease. His smile is inviting and it wraps around me like a warm blanket on our murky autumn days. I hold out my hand for a handshake. This is how the people of Talish read each other's tattoos. It's a formality to introduce yourself and to show that you are comfortable enough to reveal who you are and where you live in one gesture.

"Natsu," I say with my arm extended. But to my surprise, Taye doesn't move. He just stands there, staring at me. What is he trying to hide? I awkwardly bring my hand back to my side and look over at Karina for help. She tunes in and explains what we'll be doing for the rest of the evening which consists of dinner and a walk.

I am suddenly aware of my wardrobe choice for the day- a plain green t-shirt with a black zip-up sweater and jeans. Nothing fancy like Karina. She's in a light purple skirt with a flower pattern and white tights with a white lace top. I decide not to focus too much on my clothing choices, seeing as this is just a typical night, not a date of any kind.

We begin to walk to the restaurant and the stark difference between West Talish and the North jumps out at me. In the North, buildings are brightly coloured and there is much more agriculture and greenery around the town. Looking around, I rarely see a tree or a bush to brighten up the streets, and the colours are dark and dank, making the oncoming evening seem even murkier. It's definitely the industrial sector, metal and mechanics lining every square inch. There are many more inventions and technological advances being tested and premiering in West Talish.

Finally, after my anxiety rises distinctly from grazing past the vast array of people, we reach the restaurant. We go through the big glass doors and my eyes adjust to the dim lighting within. A beautiful lady with bright blonde hair and a great big smile welcomes us and guides us to our seats. We sit at a large booth, with Karina and I in the centre and the boys on either end of the sleek black table.

Karina and Kenjamin yap on about their lives and school woes. I sit quietly and eat a surprisingly delicious sandwich and salad, noticing that Taye keeps glancing in my direction.

"Natsu?" I startle at Karina's voice.

"Yes?"

"I said why don't you tell Taye and Kenjamin a bit about your life?

The Talish Trilogy: Changes

Maybe your family?" Poor girl, she's trying so hard.

"Yeah, sure. Um, I live in North Talish with Karina. I have a younger brother who is ten now and a younger sister whose two-years-old." It's like I'm standing in front of the class on the first day of kindergarten. The scar on my arm buzzes again under my sleeve and I instinctively raise my emotional defenses, keeping my answers vague.

"And?" Karina raises her eyebrows at me.

And? What more can I say? Her excited expression gives me pause and I let out a soft sigh. I know what she wants me to say.

"And I'm a Crafter." Immediately, Kenjamin and Taye's eyes light up with intrigue. It's a reaction I'm all too used to by now, growing up as the minority in a Mor-filled world. I'm guessing by their surprise that both Kenjamin and Taye are Mors.

"That's so cool." My eyes dart over at Taye. It has been the first words he has said. His voice is low and flows out of his lips smoothly.

"I-uh, yeah." His input takes me by surprise. This is what gets him talking?

"What kind of stuff can you do?" Kenjamin chimes in.

"Uh… regular stuff? The ordinary stuff that all Crafters can do."

What a ridiculous question.

"Can you like, make our bill disappear?" he jokes. I'm getting to know a little more about Kenjamin and his intellectual capacity.

"No, that would be stealing," I reply in more of a sarcastic tone than I intend to. Taye laughs a bit from across the table. A smile spontaneously arises on my lips and I don't know why.

"You have a beautiful smile," he says. My reddened cheeks join my unintentional body reactions and I'm just hoping they can't see it in the darkened restaurant.

"But, if you like, did a spell on the waitress to make her forget, then is it really stealing?" Kenjamin comes in with another idiotic question.

"Do you not have any money to pay the bill, Ken?" Karina asks slyly.

The Talish Trilogy: Changes

They exchange smiles and lean in for a quick kiss, allowing the awkward conversation to lay to rest.

The rest of the dinner goes more smoothly and Taye tells me about himself. I find out that he lives with his grandparents because his parents got into a car accident when he was six and passed away. He has no siblings, lucky for him, and he loves sports.

Once dinner is over, we exit into the night on the streets. Karina and Kenjamin immediately link to each other like magnets and stroll in front while Taye and I keep a few paces behind.

I look over at Taye and my heart sinks a bit, knowing that he has to spend day after day in this murky land. Why should I care though? It's not as though we're madly in love like Kenjamin and Karina. We probably won't even see each other after tonight. The idea feels like a vice has stretched around my heart, slowly tightening its grip.

"Are you okay?" I hear Taye beside me and jump a little.

"Yes, of course." I shake the thoughts from my head. "So... do you like living in West Talish?" I ask.

Taye stops me by grabbing my arm gently. His touch sends shivers up my spine and he steps towards me. My heart races and my heart beats in my ears. Was that a strange question? He then reaches his arm out towards me to indicate he wants to shake my hand. I stumble a bit, but then slowly grab it. We shake and then pause, as is custom. I look down at his tattoo and the words jump out at me: "NORTH, MORTAL". North Talish?

"You don't live here?" I let go of his hand.

He shakes his head. "I'm visiting Ken. He used to live in the North but moved a few years ago because his parents changed jobs. I come up here often to see him."

He smiles at me and I break into a laugh. I have no idea why and I feel like a complete fool when I do. Just knowing I can see him again makes me laugh like an idiot. *What is wrong with you?*

"I don't understand though, why didn't you shake my hand and show me your tattoo right away?" I ask once the idiotic giggles settle.

"Ken mentioned you were a Crafter," he explains. "I wanted to have a shot with you and I figured if you knew I was a Mor right away, I wouldn't stand a chance."

The Talish Trilogy: Changes

My heart leaps again at his comment, but also hurts at his poor self-esteem.

"I wouldn't write you off just for being a Mor," I tell him.

He shrugs. "Some girls do."

"Well, they are awfully closed-minded then. Where do you go to school?"

"North Talish High school for Mortals," he replies. Ah, a private school.

"Oh good. I'd feel awful if you went to my school and I didn't know it."

"You're at a Crafter school?" We start walking again, and I notice that Kenjamin and Karina are getting further and further away.

"No, United High," I tell him.

"Wow, your parents must be very open-minded then," he says. "My grandparents would never go for that."

"Mom," I blurt out.

"What?"

"Just my mom. My father died two years ago." I have no idea why I have decided to tell a complete stranger this intimate fact about me. Maybe it's because he told me about his parents.

"Oh, I'm very sorry." The familiar awkward atmosphere surrounds us like the cool autumn rain.

"It's fine, really. I mean, it's not fine, but it's not something I can dwell on forever. You know, with your parents- I mean… He was a Sorcerer. My dad. Him and my mom got married and got the Crafter titles of Sorcerer and Sorceress just before I was born. But… um… he—" *What are you saying? Just stop talking.*

Just as I am about to blurt out my deepest secrets like beads spilling from a jar, there's a loud scream in front of us that pierces through the conversation.

"Karina!" I gasp as Taye and I start running in the direction of the scream, pushing past a few people who have paused on the street to look in the direction of the commotion. Magic streams like a

The Talish Trilogy: Changes

rushing river into my fingertips, the familiar heat running through my veins. I find Karina standing with Kenjamin, her face pressed into his chest and he's wrapped his arms around her. I try to grab her, "Karina! What's wrong?"

Kenjamin's pale face illuminates his distress and his haunted eyes are focused on something behind me. I turn in the direction of his stare and they are looking down a nearby alley. The colour drains from my own face as I realize what he's looking at and all I can see is blood shining in the moonlight.

Joey is a writer, and professional sign language interpreter living in B.C., Canada. She graduated from the University of Victoria with a bachelor's in fine arts specializing in Theatre. She has completed five unpublished manuscripts and one self-published work. When she's not busy creating captivating content, she can be found on outings with her toddler, or at home binging a TV series (usually 90 Day Fiance or any baking show she can gets her hands on). Visit her blog www.colemanbooks.ca where you can find more samples of her writing including several short scripts she wrote for university classes and her first self-published book Marbles.

The Talish Trilogy: Changes

OFF TRACK

By Jo Ann Joseph

Jessie's shift was coming to an end. Her body told her it was quitting time hours ago. Working a double shift on the day of the Kentucky Derby was practically asking for sore feet and sciatica, but she needed the money. Derby day was the biggest money making day of the year, and that year she made a killing. Smarty Jones, a locally owned Thoroughbred, won the race, putting him in the running for the 2004 Triple Crown championship title. Bandwagon bettors from across the tri-county area swarmed the off track betting facility in droves to place their bets on the hometown hero.

A voice came from a face Jessie didn't recognize perched at her bar, "You've been polishing that same glass for like 4 minutes". He was pale, gangly, and covered in a collection of bad decisions, otherwise

Off Track

said to be tattoos. The most embarrassing of the lot being a sorry excuse for the Tasmanian Devil with the name "Mikey" scrawled in sloppy font below. A baseball cap of a team she couldn't place floated comically atop his head. His clothes hung awkwardly from his scrawny physique. He looked silly.

Jessie was only half listening. She was preoccupied with keeping watch on the front doors. Grant would be there any minute. He promised. Meanwhile, Jessie would have to acknowledge the young man on the other side of the unsolicited observation. "And you've been working on yours for like 45. Who's counting?", she quipped back. She was in no mood to play the role of friendly neighborhood barmaid. Being too amicable to a patron of the OTB was a dangerous misstep anyhow. She learned early on in her career that if you give an inch, race track rats will expect a mile.

It was nearly 10 pm, the crowd had long since dispersed but a veil of smoke still lingered in the air. Harsh fluorescent bulbs cast a sickly yellow hue on the faces of the few remaining stragglers. Most were regulars, shuffling their tickets, sipping cold coffee or warm beer, staring intently at all the pretty horses on all the shiny screens. A sea of disorderly chairs drifted in all directions from their respective tables. The sticky film of beer spilt from cheap plastic pitchers clung to soles of shoes. Little white losing tickets were crumpled in piles on cocktail tables and countertops, strewn about in every direction. Nausea washed over Jessie as she took it all in.

She took a deep breath and waited for the wave to pass. She then placed the glass she'd been so diligently polishing on a shelf. She reached for her cell phone, hoping she'd somehow missed a call or text from Grant, but no luck. Instead, the phone behind the bar let out a shrill ring. Danielle, her manager, was on the other end. "Did you make last call yet?"

"Yeah." Jessie instinctually lied.

She printed a slip from her register and handed it to the man at the bar. "Last call. I'll take that whenever you're ready." Jessie gave the building another once over; maybe there was another prescription pill pusher in her midst that she'd somehow overlooked.

The custodian, Frank, ambled about lazily sweeping discarded tickets and the occasional cigarette butt. Angie, the lone teller, was reading Marie Claire, no doubt counting the seconds for bets to close and the last pony to cross the finish line. Carla, the cocktail waitress, was by a small cluster of tables between the kitchen and bar attempting to stir Mr. Bruce from his slumber and settle his tab.

Off Track

Carla was known to dabble, but she wasn't to be trusted. Scoring drugs from a coworker that night was pretty much out of the question.

Jessie considered the customers. On any given day she could usually identify at least one person that was holding. Mr. Bruce was definitely not a drug dealer, so he was out. Mitch, a regular known for his big bets and little patience, sat in "his" seat at a high top table, finishing his 3rd and final cigar of the day. No go on that guy either. The other seating areas, surrounding the bar at the center, had cleared out hours ago. Located on the lower level, the non-smoking section, which was generally a snooze fest, and high rollers room were presumably vacant as well.

The only other patrons were Jessie's two favorites, Sid and Howard. They were in the dining room, situated at the front of the building, by the large window front. That evening, as most evenings, they sat drinking coffee while discussing art and culture. They were the last people she would ask. They were the last people she wanted to know the truth about her. She respected them, which was a rare sentiment around those parts. Jessie could hear the duo in a heated debate over Fellini and Bergman. Any fool could see that The Seventh Seal didn't hold a candle to Fellini's 8 ½. Jessie smiled, she enjoyed listening in on their conversations.

Her smile faded fast as her aching back reminded her that Grant hadn't shown up yet. She was beginning to sweat. A visceral anxiety built in the pit of her stomach. Soon, the aches would become more than a gentle reminder. Her guts would start to bubble and froth. Her muscles would spasm, trying to break free from the torture of her own skin. Once she left that building the chances of connecting with Grant decreased exponentially. Where the hell was he? More importantly, she wondered, where the hell was *she*? How had she ended up this way? If only that drunken idiot hadn't T-boned her at 8 in the morning all those months ago. Why hadn't her doctors prepared her for how awful she would feel once she was off the meds? Or, how amazing she would feel on them? She told herself she was going to beat this thing. She'd set it all right, just not tonight.

Jessie continued to meticulously clean her bar, doing her best to stall until Grant showed up. Every few seconds, she returned her gaze to the window front in search of his headlights. In the glow of the street lights illuminating the near empty parking lot she noticed the wind kicking up debris in the air. A storm was coming, only further complicating her situation. She watched the front door, maybe he'd come strolling in. At least someone was watching, she thought, as she took a moment to observe Duane, the unarmed rent-a-cop manning his post in a chair next to the entryway. An old

Off Track

metal sign for Gamblers Anonymous, complete with a 1-800 line, hung on the wall above his head. He looked one long blink away from joining the ranks of Mr. Bruce in public slumberland. Jessie's eyes nearly rolled out of her head as she scoffed at the lame excuse for security.

She'd finished cleaning up when she spotted her manager, Danielle, behind the teller line, next to Angie. She motioned to Jessie, discreetly as possible, to wrap it up. Just as Jessie walked over to the man at the bar to collect his debt her ears perked to the familiar sound of doors opening. Her eyes shot up toward the front of the building as she let out what should have been a sigh of relief. Only it wasn't. The man walking through the doorway was not the one she had been anticipating. He was quite the opposite.

People sometimes called him Salt, but nicknames were common for guys who frequented the racetrack. She didn't know his actual name, only his face, and the uneasy feeling that came along with it. He always wore fresh Jordan's, with basketball shorts and a bright white tee, creating a stark contrast to his onyx skin. He stood an intimidating 6"6', with a wide frame and permanent scowl. The way he looked at Jessie made her uncomfortable. The comments he made about her appearance, in his thick patois accent, made her angry. She thought she ought to give him a good slap across his big stupid face. She would need to borrow the step stool from the kitchen for that. Instead, she kept it to herself, smiled politely and practiced avoidance whenever possible. Above all, Jessie was scared of him. Rumor had it that he was recently banned from the OTB for an alleged stabbing incident in the parking lot. "This night keeps getting better, doesn't it?"she mumbled to herself.

She proceeded with collecting the money now present on the bar. "Keep the change", said Looney Tunes Mikey, as he had been christened in Jessie's mind. She did not bother to give thanks for the unimpressive $0.35. No matter, people were much more generous earlier in the day. Also, she pilfered a decent sum of cash by shorting the register all day. She turned her back to gather her things and settle her till for the day. "Psst, psst…yo, Shorty…", Mikey called to her. Annoyed, she swung around to find him buzzing with a nervous energy. He was tapping something on the countertop of the bar. A small black handgun. "I'm actually gonna need that back". He tossed a backpack across the bar, hitting Jessie in the face.

This goober was about to take all the tips she'd earned over the past 12 hours. Just great! She had a measly $18.23 in her bank account. The thought of having to ask her dad for help again wrenched her already churning stomach. And what for the expensive habit of keeping herself well? Hopefully, Grant would just spot her the pills

Off Track

until she could pay him back.

She began to empty the contents of her register into the bag and noticed from the corner of her eye Danielle and Angie in a similar predicament. The scary man known as Salt was pointing a Glock 17 from his hip in their direction. He handed them a large duffel bag she hadn't noticed when he walked in. They were communicating in hushed voices, so Jessie couldn't make out what was being said. Danielle briefly locked eyes with Jessie, attempting meaningful exchange. Jessie was unsure if the slight shift of her brow was meant to communicate reassurance or the fact that they were fucked.

In an act of absolute imperfect timing the doors swung open again, tornado like winds blowing Grant into the vestibule. In that very instant sirens could be heard in the near distance. Salt must have recognized the face from around the club because he didn't shoot Grant on sight. He turned back to Danielle, "You press di alarm?"

Danielle shook her head with a vigorous no. He raised his gun to her eye level, "Lock di door." Danielle froze, tears streaming down her face. Salt, thrust the gun toward her, "Bomboclat! Lakk it up!" Danielle carefully climbed over the teller line, barely holding back hysteria, and did as she was told.

Bardsy 2023 Fall Anthology — First Chapters

People started to rise from seated positions to see what the hell was going on. Jessie looked at the young man currently holding her at gunpoint. As he watched his plan start to crumble rather than unfold, all confidence drained from his sun starved face. Jessie could see a disquiet flood his wild eyes. Then, the thud of 200 lbs of flesh hitting the tiled floor put pause to the chaos. Duane, who had indeed dozed off on the job, was startled by all the commotion and fell from his chair.

Mikey jumped from his bar stool at the sound. He was scared. So scared, in fact, that he took his Hi-point pistol, in what can only be loosely referred to as aim, and fired in the general direction of the perceived threat. Mikey, it seemed, had lied on his resume when applying for this job. He had never handled, much less shot a gun before he purchased one out of the trunk of an Oldsmobile 3 days prior. Everyone in the building, Mr. Bruce and Salt excluded, hit the deck when the deafening blast reverberated off the high ceilings. Duane was already on the floor, only now, he was sitting upright, in a pool of his own blood, clutching the left side of his body.

Jessie turned away from the bloody heap of a man she had sneered at only minutes before. The sight was more than she could stomach. His cries of pain nearly drowned out the intense ringing in her ears. There was a smell, too. Jessie couldn't decide if it was that of fresh

Off Track

blood, or the mass amounts of cortisol being produced by the men responsible. She could see it in their eyes. Everyone could. The armed robbers were panicking, which is generally not a preferable scenario. As demonstrated by Mikey, jittery fingers drop balls. Or in this case, pull triggers and shoot innocent, sleepy eyed bystanders. A loaded gun in the hands of a nervous man is a very dangerous thing. They were dealing with two.

Philadelphia native, Jo Ann Joseph is a licensed veterinary nurse, also formally trained in the art of taxidermy. When not caring for animals or embarrassing her husband and 2 daughters, she spends her time consuming horror in every form of media. She started off writing scripts and music for a local burlesque troupe and now writes stories inspired by her own life experiences with a uniquely dark twist. Currently, she is working on a collection of allegorical horror shorts based on the pathophysiology of terminal illnesses.

Off Track

THE PRIVATEER

Paula Bryner

The last cannon was fired and its black powder smoke, with the blue sheen of gunmetal, curled up toward the radiant sky. The acrid, saltpeter smell burned eyes and noses. All around aboard the prize ship, men were being herded together in anticipation of their unpleasant future in the hold of their own vessel. Watching these prisoners of her captain, Juliette reminded herself that fear was her worst enemy. This time she would take command.

"Is all well below, Hubert?" She called out to her ship's bosun above the last ring of gunfire.

"It is." He nodded, his long, equine face wearing a sneer.

"Lieutenant."

The Privateer

Juliette ignored the familiar tone in Hubert's voice. After two years as First aboard her lover's ship, she knew all too well that the men of *Sociere* disliked taking orders from a woman. They loved a prize ship, though, and the money in their pockets once it paid off. A woman barking at them could be tolerated if the ship was rich enough. This one was.

"The women are on their way to our ship?"

"As you ordered." Hubert's snide tone made a few of his shipmates chuckle.

"Very well." Juliette pointed to the merchant crew, huddled together like sheep in a branding pen with their eyes wide and their bodies sinewy from years of punishing work. "Take those men to the hold and lock them up. The rest of you, I'll need volunteers with me to see this ship into port."

"What volunteers, then?" Faroud, *Sorciere*'s coxswain and a man notorious for his cruelty, looked Juliette up and down. Her sailor's shirt and loose trousers did very little to conceal the curves of her body. "You will captain her into Barataria?"

"And so I shall." Juliette drew herself up to her full height, which was impressive even among the men gathered around her. She pitched her voice to be heard, and to carry a confidence she did not altogether feel.

Juliette was taking a calculated risk, and this time she would do everything possible to see it pay off just like the prize beneath her bare feet. "Certainly Captain D'Armound will choose to continue in the Gulf. Who wants another prize more than our captain, I have to ask?"

The men around her thought about this possibility. Some even went so far as to nod their agreement.

"So hurry now to your duty. The order has been given. Let us – "

"Lieutenant Flynn." Louis Antoine D'Armound's booming voice echoed over the blue water around the ship as he appeared from below.

Juliette's heart leapt in her chest. Since 1805, D'Armound had been the most successful sea raider out of the south Louisiana privateer base known as Barataria Bay. Now, a short four years later, his vessel was

The Privateer

feared and avoided by merchantmen and navy ships alike. His temper was legendary. Juliette braced herself to feel its full force.

"What is it that you are doing?" D'Armound stepped to his First Lieutenant, piercing through to her soul with his black, bird of prey eyes. He crossed his muscular arms over his chest and continued to stare.

Juliette wanted to wince, to shrink back and try to disappear. This time though, she would not. She took in the freshening breeze that was the only sound on deck. Everyone around her stared at Captain D'Armound in quiet fear or anticipation, depending on their attitude.

"I asked you a question, Mademoiselle." His voice was like gravel on a wooden deck as he just opened his thin lips to speak through his teeth.

"Did not you wisely intend to take the prize into Barataria, Monsieur?" She cursed herself for sounding conciliatory and anxious. Years of abuse at home taught Juliette that the best way to avoid a blow was to flatter the man with his fist clenched. "Could not that be accomplished by me, with a small crew, while you hunt more prey here in the Gulf of Mexico?"

"I've no intention of putting you in charge of this ship." His posture relaxed, if only a bit.

"Of course not." She smiled and reached out to him, taking his shifting body language as an opportunity.

"But cannot intentions change? If you allow me to make for Bartaria with your prize, I can begin negotiating the sale of her cargo through Laffite before ever you think to follow us with yet more merchants in tow. Does not that appeal, Monsieur?"

"You think you could do so much then?" His gaze drifted to her long-fingered hand just at his elbow, touching him like the breeze.

"I am certain of it." Her eyes, the color of Baltic amber, lit up with the promise of a ship to command.

Even if that ship was in her charge only temporarily. "Try me. Give me this chance."

D'Armound smiled his crooked, unreadable smile. Then, before anyone saw it coming, he backhanded his First Lieutenant across

The Privateer

the left side of her head.

Juliette fell to the deck, her body hitting the hard wood with a painful thump. She sniffed, feeling the blood drip from her left nostril. The ringing in her ears deafened her to the hurried sounds all around. As men turned to whatever duty they could find in a frenzy to avoid their captain's rage, she shook her head trying to see straight again.

"I should say, Monsieur." Benoit St. Louis, Juliette's friend and mentor during her time aboard *Sorciere*, stepped between D'Armound and the Lieutenant. "Nothing will be accomplished in this manner. Prize crews diminish a privateer's effectiveness, sure, but the point is well taken. You could hunt yet more, even with a smaller company."

"Do not you badger me as well, Leadsman." D'Armound glanced at Juliette who was still crumpled on the deck just behind Benoit. "Hubert, take those merchant sailors below. You will helm this ship and follow us into Barataria where I will see to the disposal of her cargo. Any man not selected to crew this ship, back to

Sorciere now. That includes Lieutenant Flynn."

"As you say, Monsieur." St. Louis gave a bow as the captain brushed past him. Then, when he was certain that D'Armound was on his way back to their ship, Benoit knelt at Juliette's side.

"Here now, ma'am." Ty Brayton was helping her to a seated position. Formerly enslaved, Ty was now a free man who worked aboard *Sorciere* as a common sailor. He too was a close friend of the First Lieutenant.

"You gonna be all right?"

"I..." Juliette ran the back of her hand under her nose and was not surprised at the crimson blood that spotted her tan skin. The viscous, milk-warm feeling made her wipe her hand on her shirt. "I shall be."

"You cannot continue like this," Benoit said in an under voice. His keen, viridian eyes continued to watch D'Armound while he spoke. "This shameful treatment must stop."

"He treats us all so, Ben." Juliette glanced up with a rueful chuckle that had no mirth to it. "Ever since Laffite became bos at Barataria, Louis hates every man jack aboard all ships, including his. He hates himself most of all."

The Privateer

"That doesn't give him the right to strike you." Ty looked closely at Juliette. When he saw the focus return to her eyes, he asked: "Ready to stand up?"

She nodded, unsure but willing to try. Her friends hoisted her to her feet and Juliette managed to steady herself. "I am well."

"It is time to run," Ben said with a frown. "We cannot watch him do this to you."

"Where would I go, Ben?" Juliette shook her head, regretting the action when she felt dizzy again.

"I cannot return home to Carolina. I've told you about my brother."

"Of course not but there are those of us who would join you in your exodus." Ben tried to pitch his voice to encourage. He didn't want Juliette to know that his concern for her was almost overwhelming. "Those with no love for D'Armound at all."

"I know." Juliette looked from Ben to Ty. "And I am fortunate in my friends, but my own ship is not going to materialize through wishing, is it? I need more time to husband my funds. Please, do you trust me in this. Within the hour our captain will be a lamb again, and sorry for raising his hand in anger."

"Come along, Lieutenant Flynn." Faroud was calling from the ship's rail, a nasty tone in his voice.

"Boat's leaving for *Sorciere* and the Captain grows impatient for his supper."

"I am there." Juliette took in a deep breath and looked to her friends. "Thank you indeed. Do not you worry. We will be free of this service soon enough." With a nod and a smile, she left them behind to climb over the rail and descend the rope ladder down to the little gig that would take her back to D'Armound's ship.

***

As the sun disappeared into the western horizon, First Lieutenant Flynn commenced to transform into Mademoiselle Juliette in the confines of the coach. This was a small pantry outside the captain's cabin with a drapery for modesty. She splashed herself with the sweet water provided and donned the gown Louis left for her. Her black curls were worn in the daring Titus fashion made popular in France, cut short and allowed to frame her face naturally. Her limbs were scented with rose oil.

"There you are now, Juliette." Louis smiled when she entered the cabin. He raised her hand to his lips and they lingered on her palm. "How very lovely you do look."

"*Merci.*" She curtsied, glancing at the table in the center of the small room. Supper was out on the white cloth where silver trays and trenchers sparkled in the orange glow of two ship's lanterns. "Are we expecting royalty?"

"You are my royalty, without a doubt." Louis picked up a bottle.

"Oh, champagne."

"Hubert found it aboard the prize. Shall we toast?"

"Most assuredly."

"To success then, eh? And to Juliette Flynn, the loveliest First Lieutenant in the Gulf." They drank, and Louis watched her over the rim of his glass. "Do you like it?"

"It is a delightful vintage."

"Captain Mendoza evidently knows his wine, if very little else."

"You don't think much of him, do you?"

"I would prefer not to think on him at all. Particularly right now." He cleared his throat and drank his glass empty. "I am sorry for what happened today, truly. You know I should never like to hurt you but you push me, Juliette. You push me too damn hard."

She nodded, keeping her expression neutral. The speech was familiar and she hoped it was over.

"Oh, and here." Louis was suddenly full of good cheer as he produced a carved, mahogany box. "I desire this truly delights you."

"A gift?" Despite herself, she felt a wave of anticipation. A pleasant surprise was a welcome distraction from the general monotony of shipboard life.

"Just what you deserve."

Juliette held the wooden box a moment, looking at the intricate joinery that made each little piece fit together like the hull of a ship.

The Privateer

"Will you not open it?"

She smiled at him and shrugged, then she pushed back the lid of the box. Inside were twelve yellow topaz studs that winked at her in the lantern light. Her smile fell away as she ran her fingers over the beautiful, brilliant cut gems.

"Are they not to your liking?" His voice was filled with honest concern.

"Louis." She looked up at him after a long pause. Her amber eyes, like the jewels, glinted in the light.

"They are enchanting."

"A brace of topaz, straight out of the captain's cabin. Mendoza knows jewels as well, apparently." Louis reached for the bottle and helped himself to more champagne.

"You may have them set any way you like when we reach the city. I will see to it personally."

"I am overwhelmed."

He watched her look at the jewels for a time, her enjoyment in their beauty feeding his pride. "Then I am well satisfied. Dillon." Louis called for his steward. The discussion of women's things was over. "The first course now."

The old steward served the soup while Louis helped Juliette into her chair. She picked up her spoon with a generous smile as he joined her at table.

"Juliette," he said once Dillon was gone. "You are a vision in the lantern light and no mistake. More champagne?"

"Oh please."

As he finished his pour, Louis was distracted by voices outside his cabin. "What is that now?" He frowned toward the door.

"Who can say?" Juliette tittered like a debutante, knowing this behavior would keep him calm. "The men are anxious to be by land. Thank you so much for the lovely evening, Monsieur."

"It is my pleasure. I could not – What the hell is that?" Louis' gaze turned once again to the cabin door as the voices beyond increased

The Privateer

in volume.

Louis' steward appeared at tableside once again. Anxiety creased his leathery visage as he crept to his captain and bent to Louis' ear.

As Dillon whispered, Louis stared at Juliette. By agonizing degrees, his face contorted into an angry grimace. Finally he rose to his feet, nearly knocking old Dillon over, and barked at his Lieutenant: "This is unacceptable."

"My word, Monsieur." Juliette stood too, honest confusion causing her eyes to drift away from Louis toward the cabin door. "Whatever can I do to correct your disapprobation?"

"Let them enter, Dillon." Louis was still watching Juliette. "It is apparently necessary to show the Lieutenant her grievous error."

Juliette felt a sick, emetic taste in her mouth as two of Louis' officers marched Ty Brayton and one of the young ladies in Juliette's charge into the great cabin. Both looked as if they had been manhandled already. Ty's face was bruised and the woman's calico gown did not quite drop to her ankles, leaving her calves bare. Juliette tried to swallow her horror, feeling hopeless at the scene before her.

"Basanez," Louis said to the man who was holding the young woman by the arm. "Explain to Lieutenant Flynn what this is about."

"We caught them together." Felix Basanez began while leering at Juliette. "If you take my meaning."

"I take it very well." Louis turned his attention to Ty. "You've sailed with me these two years gone, Brayton. You know the rule of this ship."

"Well?" Sylvain Delhomme, the ship's Master, shook Ty's arm when he did not reply to the captain.

"Have you no explanation, boy?"

"It will do no good." Ty lisped around his swelling, purple lower lip.

"No." Juliette came back to herself at last. She hurried to Louis' side, trying to take his hand.

"No, Monsieur. Clearly there is some misunderstanding. Brayton would never go against your orders, much less hurt a woman with malice. It is not his nature."

"You are the one mistaken, Lieutenant." Louis looked her up and down as if she were an insect who had just crawled out of his food. "And I am Captain D'Armound to you."

Juliette nodded as she glanced at Ty.

"The rule has been broken and the punishment is known to every man aboard us." Louis made his pronouncement in a quarterdeck voice that echoed off the low ceiling of the cabin. "Take this sailor and put him in bilboes below. Tomorrow it is forty off your back with a heavy cat, and there should be no surprise in that."

"None," Ty said in a low, defiant voice. "Sir."

"And the girl?" Basanez exchanged an arch look with Delhomme as he spoke.

"I've no concern for it." Louis now spoke casually, as if he were discussing a piece of clothing or a wheel of cheese. "That is tainted goods now that Brayton's manhandled her. Do with her as you wish."

"Oh no Captain, please." Juliette resumed her argument, no longer concerned with the consequences to herself. "You know what will come of this. Let me take the woman back to her people. I will lock them in, I promise. Whatever pleases you, but not this."

"I said enough." Louis did not trouble himself to glance at Juliette as he continued to speak. His hand though, like the iron bilboes that would chain Ty to the planking of the ship, closed tight around her wrist. "Leave my cabin, all of you."

The exit from the captain's presence was over in a hurry. Even old Dillon slipped out of the simmering space, closing the door behind him. Juliette was left alone with her angry oppressor. Her skin tingled as if it had been touched by ice while her mind filled with horrible dread. The silence, which was surrounded by the sounds of ocean and wind, was like being encased in an airless vacuum.

"I will see to your punishment myself, Lieutenant, as is only seemly. You retreat now to the sleeping cabin and wait for me." Louis looked at her, anger radiating from his body like the heat of a stove. He let go of her wrist, leaving a red welt on her tan skin.

Juliette bit her lip, gave a formal curtsy and moved to the dim of the sleeping cabin. She stood next to the cot in a familiar position, her trepidation growing with each silent moment. Behind her anxiety, though, a subtle but strong voice kept repeating in her head: "Time to run. Time to run. Endure this, and then run."

Writing for over 30 years, I have at least 300 years of seafaring adventure in my family history. My own adventures include time in most of the US and Mexico as well as six months in Haiti as a research assistant. I'm a word nerd and I have never given up on the passion for history instilled in me by my Creole Dad, John Richard. I hold a degree in Anthropology and continue my learning journey as a member of the Alaska Writers' Guild and 49 Writers, Alaska. Find me on the web @paulineagain on Twitter/X or Paula Bryner on Facebook.

The Privateer

Printed in Great Britain
by Amazon